Pennance

by Clare Ashton

Copyright © Clare Ashton 2012

All characters appearing in this work are fictitious. Any resemblance to real persons, living or dead, is purely coincidental.

All rights reserved

First edition

Part 1
1.

They were looking at me. I didn't need to look up and around the store to know that. The village supermarket was too quiet for people actively shopping. No-one was shuffling around the aisles, browsing for their goods. No-one talked. I could imagine them peering over the shelves towards me.

A woman whispered on the other side of the shop. 'Such a shame.' I closed my eyes, trying not to blush at the familiar attention. It used to be 'Such a shame. Such a lovely young couple. She is young though,' as if I had plenty of time and strength to recover.

Now, a year later, it was just 'Such a shame'.

I made myself concentrate on the tins of soup on the shelf in front of me. I needed one for each day for lunch. Tomato, mushroom, chicken. I put one of each in my basket. I stared at the other choices, like I always did, and took another can each of tomato, mushroom and chicken. I needed one more to last the week.

My mind went blank with indecision under the scrutiny of the onlookers. I read the labels of the cans in front of me, but the words wouldn't stay in my head long enough for me to decide. I didn't know what to do. I could feel my heartbeat thud in my chest and the grip that strangled my stomach start to work its way up. I had to move on. I would have to miss lunch that day.

I moved towards the back of the shop. There was a convex mirror up in the corner by the ceiling. I appeared large in it, distorted with a huge head, my body disappearing to tiny feet. Even through the distortion I could see that I didn't look the same.

I had never bothered with much makeup. Now I no longer bothered at all. My face was uniformly pale, undulating plainly over my cheeks with horizontal impassive lines for eyebrows and a mouth. I had my hair tied back which made me look more featureless. I was stooping, cowering over my basket. I could feel that I was drawing people's attention the more I tried to hide. I couldn't stand up straight and confident though.

I could see two women by the tills in the exaggerated distance. Their tiny faces were turned, looking towards me. Perhaps they didn't think that I could see them. 'Such a shame. Such a lovely young couple,' I heard one say at last. One of the tiny heads shook from side to side. I couldn't tell whether it was the one that had spoken or the other responding in agreement.

They were old, I could see that. What I called old. They would have to be to have considered us a young couple. I was still youthful, all of twenty-six, but Jake had been forty. We had been together for three years. Perhaps that's what they meant by a young couple.

I moved on, feeling them turn and following me with their looks around the store. I tried not to listen. I picked up two loaves of bread and seven packets of noodles. I thought I should look for something else, some more variety that I could boil, microwave or toast, but I had taken too much time already. I picked up three large cartons of milk and a handful of chocolate bars and walked up to the other till, trying not to look towards the women.

I held my breath and stared down while I lifted the food onto the conveyor belt. I didn't want to see the look of recognition from the person at the till. I was avoiding the look of pity that would follow: the tilting of the head, the pursed lips, the upturned eyebrows. It would only encourage the grip around my stomach, make it rise and choke the tears out of me, make me start to convulse and shake with fear, scared of all that pity that I didn't deserve.

I packed my rucksack and two carrier bags and paid in cash without looking up. It was nearly nine o'clock when I left the shop and I was running late.

It was twilight outside, still and overcast. It was the end of October and the days did not become properly light when the weather was bad. The Devonian slate shops and houses around the village green looked dark and wet. The air was moist from the incessant drizzle and the clouds that crawled up the valley from the sea. The buildings looked like miserable animals today, all huddled around the village green with nothing better to do.

I looked up the road that went inland. Jake's mother would walk down that street any moment on her way to work at the post office. I dreaded seeing that characteristic walk: the slightly dropped shoulders carrying her shopping bag, the blue nylon comfortable trousers, the red woollen overcoat stretched tight around her middle that clashed so badly with her greying auburn hair. I could imagine her so vividly through my anxiety that I had to blink several times to clear her image from the empty street. I opened my eyes wide, so that they felt cold in the breeze, trying to force them to adjust to reality.

I saw the empty street for a moment and then a small red figure appeared in the distance, on the horizon, stepping out from one of the white-washed cottages at the edge of the village.

My chest and throat clenched, throttling out a gurgle of distress. Tears filled my eyes and a sob escaped my mouth, despairing at the timing. I ran across the street to my bike that was locked to a bench on the edge of the green. My hands were shaking as I tried to unlock it, the two plastic carrier bags swinging and rolling in the way. My fingers were numb and a deep pain rang through my knuckles as I wrenched the lock apart and knocked my hand against a pedal.

The lock slipped from my wet fingers and fell noisily on the pavement. I almost burst into tears. I was tempted to leave the bike, the shopping and the lock and walk away.

Put the bags down, I told myself, having to think every separate word of the instruction to make myself calm. Pick up the lock. Now put the lock in the carrier bag. Better. Step over the bar and sit on the seat. Now push on the pedal.

The bike wobbled beneath me as I peddled away from the green, the two carrier bags swinging either side of the front wheel. I pushed down hard on the pedal, my legs feeling weak with the nervous exertion. It wasn't far to the single-track road that would take me out of the village towards the sea. I should make it. I mustn't look back.

'Lucy!' I heard. It was an unmistakeable voice, and I heard it clearly even though the sound was dulled by the mist. 'Lucy!' she cried again. But I had turned into the lane and the bike had gathered speed down the hill. My neck felt stiff, locked forward unwilling to turn around and catch sight of her.

*

I started to breathe easier as the bike free-wheeled past the last house in the village and down the hill. I thought I could smell the sea on the way home. I don't think I could, especially on a day like that when my nose was numb with cold.

The road ran down a spur that struck out to the sea. You could peer over the hedges and across the fields that time of year. The fields to the south were dotted with sheep, white in the distance but a dirty cream closer up. Some looked at me as I wobbled past on my bike, staring at me with wide eyes that didn't look real: big, uncomprehending, glass marbles. They unnerved me, stretching up their necks, agitated, and looking down at me.

I wobbled on the bike again, a tin in a carrier bag jumping in and out of the spokes. I swore. I should have brought the bigger rucksack, or perhaps risked walking. There were fewer people around this time of year; no-one to stop when they recognised me, wanting to offer me a lift, thinking it kind.

I was only likely to pass the farmer that time of year. He understood not to stop now. He'd been persistent and uncomprehending in his offer of a lift in his Land Rover. I'd had to shout at him to refuse. He'd looked offended and disconcerted at how adamant I had been. He looked embarrassed whenever he passed now. Perhaps someone had explained to him how inappropriate it had been to try to force me into a car again.

I only had to cycle half a mile before turning off the road into a lane to my house. The lane dropped into a wooded valley that ran all the way from the sea up to Pennance. I lived half way between the two.

The valley looked dark. The bare trees were black, their trunks and branches sodden with moisture. They looked eerily frozen on either side of the lane as I cycled down to the cottage. They looked like they were pretending to stand still, waiting to pounce. I could imagine them turning to look, behind me, as I cycled past.

It was darkest on this side of the valley, even though there were no leaves in the wood canopy by then. The sun didn't get high enough in the sky that time of year to peer over the curving sides of the valley. The air was still and moist and soaking green moss carpeted the area around the cottage. It was a relief to wheel up to the front door. I'd made it home and I expected not to see anyone for another week.

The cottage was an old, white-washed stone building that must have been intended for farm labourers. Further up the lane, in the centre of the valley was a larger Georgian house that would have been the main farm house. It had been empty since the elderly couple that lived there had died the year before last and no-one would pass down the lane for weeks at a time.

I didn't bother locking up the bike. I wheeled it down the side of the cottage, and leant it against the logs under the shelter that backed into the earth behind the house. I put down my bags and felt around my jeans pockets to find the long mortice key. I looked up at the door. I couldn't see through the glass. My house looked dark and unlived in too. I could only see my reflection, reaching out, as I put the key into the keyhole.

The house was colder than outside, still retaining the chill from the night. Its musty air enveloped me as I stepped through the door, brushing my face, making it clammy. I shut the door behind me, silencing the hushing sounds of the distant breaking sea. The house was quiet. The silence made my ears feel stiff and strained. I waited for a moment with my eyes closed, feeling the cold, moist air on my eyelids. I was waiting for Jake to appear.

He always seemed to appear behind me. His presence would make my skin prickle down my neck, shoulders and back. A cushion of cold air would seem to touch me, gently brushing across my back, as he formed behind me. I would hear him breathe, almost smell him. He always smelled of fresh perspiration to me.

He only trailed me around the house, he never followed me outdoors. I would think of him away from home, he hardly left my thoughts. But I never thought of him as clearly as I did in the cottage. When I reached back I expected him to take my hand, my fingers tingling with the expectation of contact with his large, fleshy hands.

He didn't appear at that moment. I opened my eyes to the empty dark kitchen. It was a mess. It had been a mess for a year. The dining table in the middle of the room had piles of post: paid bills, unopened offers, letters for Jake. The back of the kitchen hadn't been disturbed for months. The gas cooker was covered with pans from the last meal I had cooked before the gas canister ran out. I was too afraid to replace it afterwards.

I only used the small surface by the window. I used the microwave, kettle and toaster and the sink to wash up the single set of cutlery, a mug and a plate. I would sometimes stare out of the window while I washed them. I would find myself leaning on my straightened arms, my hands wrist-deep in cold water, all the bubbles from the washing up liquid popped, leaving soapy round outlines up my arms. I'm not sure what I thought of while I stared; nothing most of the time.

I emptied out my rucksack and bags, lining up the soups and noodles by day on the top. The fridge needed cleaning I noticed when I put away the milk. It still smelled of some soft cheese that I had bought last year.

I scrunched up the plastic bags and threw them under the table. They rustled and tumbled on the stone floor. It looked filthy. I couldn't remember the last time I had cleaned it. It had a thin spongy layer of dirt on it, a mixture of mud, food and anything else I had walked in. It had reached a stage where it wouldn't look any dirtier, and I was happy to leave it that way.

I turned my back on it and turned up the narrow stairs between the kitchen and living room, climbing up into the light. My bedroom was at the front of the house, overlooking the lane and into the trees. I could see through the low window from the landing. The glass panes were warped with condensation that pooled on the window ledge. The trees outside moved as I walked into the room, their branches rippling across the streams of moisture as I swayed from side to side, stepping into the bedroom.

The ceiling was low and divided by a large black beam. I felt oversized, a tall, modern woman in a house made for workers on a more moderate diet. I thought of Jake stooping, ducking under the beam when getting into the double bed by the window. The ingrained memory of him, stooping and then sitting on the bed, swinging his long muscled legs over, seemed to summon him.

I could feel him standing behind me. I imagined his cold breath on the top of my head. He was a tall man. He had been a tall man. I thought of him looking down on me, breath coming from his nostrils. He would be standing there, his strong arms crossed in front of his barrel chest. It was a stance that I associated with all policemen now.

He had auburn hair like his mother, and that pale chicken skin that people with red hair have. It wasn't unattractive, just strangely tender for covering a big hulk of a man.

I imagined turning round, stepping into his arms and resting my head on his firm chest. He would squeeze me gently and rest his chin on the top of my head. He would tell me that everything was all right, if I let him speak, despite what I had done. I imagined him reconciled to what had happened. It was my own guilt and other's opinions that made me afraid.

'Sorry, I must get on with some work,' I thought uncomfortably, remembering my guilt.

I changed, swapping the jeans covered in mud and oil from the bike for a clean pair. I sloughed off my waterproof jacket on to the floor and peeled my cold, sweaty T-shirt over my head.

Out of habit I scratched my forearm, around the long scar that ran towards my hand. I stroked my finger along its length. It felt smooth and plump. It looked like a huge earthworm, flattened and stuck on my arm. I imagined Jake's cold presence reaching round and touching it too, stroking my arm in a light caress. I wished I could take his hand in mine, show him not to worry, that it didn't bother me at all. It felt odd realising what the car accident had left and what it had taken away.

I was beginning to shiver and prickle with goose bumps. I quickly put on a couple of fleece tops and thick socks and went downstairs to the sitting room. I had to put the light on. The room only had one window, out onto the passage down the side of the house, and it was the darkest room in the house. It looked empty with the vacant sofa facing the bare fireplace. There were few other things in the room apart from my desk and computer, stuck between the back of the sofa and the window. It was cold in there too. I switched on the oil heater, turning it up to full before sitting at my desk.

I had left my computer on standby so that I could work immediately if I could. I couldn't cope with eight hours solid of work. I had fragmented days, sleeping, working and eating when I could rather than when I should.

I checked my email. Work had sent a late design change for the web site I was updating. My boss had written the request in the gentlest way possible, not to cause me any anxiety about the urgency of the work. His considerate words made me feel guilty.

I replied to him, promising to check in the web site code to the company software repository by the end of the weekend. My mind had started thinking about the changes I needed to make, eager to solve the programming puzzle.

I stopped. Jake had arrived. I could feel him standing behind me. I thought he rested his cold hands on my shoulders, looking over my head at the screen.

'I can't work with you there,' I thought, apologising, thinking the words clearly to him. 'I'm going to work for a while.'

I covered my ears with my headphones. Music broke him up, dissipating the cold feeling behind me. It helped me concentrate, cancelling out other distractions, cocooning me in familiar sounds. I started to think, my eyes becoming blurred, imagining the shape of the software.

2.

There was a face at the window, a man's face, dark and unshaven. The edge of his hand was pressed smooth against the glass, shading his eyes. His breath clouded his image for a moment and then it reappeared. His eyes glistened beneath black waves of hair and were fixed on mine.

I sat staring at him, feeling the warmth of my body drain away in fright. My mouth had dropped open and my eyes were stretched wide with shock. My heart beat so hard against the front of my chest that it felt like it must be visible, pulsing and rising under my skin.

I did not recognise him immediately. The fright paralysed my mind as well as my body. In front of me, the man's mouth opened and contorted around his sentences, his dark red tongue moving behind a row of yellow teeth that bit over the words. It looked frightening, disgusting, without being able to hear the sound.

It was Tom Riley from the garage. I felt sick with the recognition. I had a pile of his letters on the kitchen table, each more desperate than the previous, pleading with me to settle out of court and end the negligence case as quickly as possible.

I snapped off my headphones and stood up quickly, my chair scraping noisily on the floor as I pushed it backwards. 'Mrs Arundell,' I heard him say in a thick rural accent. It seemed to me that he growled the words, rolling guttural sounds in his throat.

I stepped away from my desk towards the stairs. He mirrored my movement, moving along the house towards the front door. I suppose he thought that I was walking to the kitchen and that I was going to let him in. I froze again in panic, holding the back of the chair.

He reappeared at the window. 'Mrs Arundell. I knocked on your door like. I didn't think you could hear me.' I could hear him, but I didn't take in what he said.

I felt sick and cornered. Without thought, I darted towards the stairs and leapt up the steps until I was halfway. I turned around to check that I was hidden. I could see his blurred shadow move on the floor as he walked from the lounge window, along the wall to the kitchen and then back again. He seemed like an animal to me, prowling round the house, trying to find a way in.

A sob of desperation escaped my mouth when I realised the front door wasn't locked. I sank back onto the step, and started to curl up smaller, holding my knees and pulling them to my face.

'I just want to talk to you. Please. Mrs Arundell.' I could hear his voice break higher, exasperated. His shadow stopped outside the lounge. 'People don't come to the garage no more,' he pleaded. 'Please Mrs Arundell. I just want to sort things out.'

I sat huddled on the stairs. My throat was constricted and tight. I let out a strangled groan as I pulled myself tighter into a ball.

'I've got rid of the bloke who worked on your car. I've retrained everyone else. I'm trying to do the right thing. Please Mrs Arundell. I've told my solicitor to up the offer but he says you won't listen.'

I was starting to feel strange and distant. I closed my eyes and felt surrounded by a comforting soft darkness. I seemed to rock with the strong beat of my heart. It made my head twitch involuntarily, backwards and then forwards, ticking. I didn't hear what he said after that, although he carried on shouting and prowling back and forth.

I saw the night of the accident instead. It played out often in my head. No-one would ever let me forget it, from the police on the scene to the solicitor who Jake's family had hired, over and over again.

We were almost home. We'd been camping on Dartmoor, catching the last of the dry weather last September. I was tired, a little cold. It was late at night and very dark, with all the stars visible.

We were coming down the hill a mile from Pennance. I heard a sound from underneath the car: a mixture of a thud and sharper sound of metal. 'What was that?' I said, not particularly concerned. I was too tired to worry about it properly. I turned to Jake. He pursed his lips and raised his eyebrows, shrugging unconcerned too.

We broke over the brow of a hill and tipped down the narrow road lined with trees. The trunks shone grey on either side of the road in the headlights, stretching branches above us, forming a tunnel around the road.

Another car blinked around the corner a hundred metres or so in front of us, switching from full beam to dipped. Jake shifted down a gear and lifted his foot to the brake. His foot stamped on the floor, the pedal offering no resistance. He looked down alarmed. Again and again his foot stamped on the floor. 'Shit' I heard him say. I looked at him, panic rising in me. I saw him straighten his arms, pushing him away from the steering wheel. His face looked pale in the bright car lights coming towards us.

*

'No. Please,' I cried. I pleaded that the flood of memories would stop. I was breathing quickly and heavily in panic. I was shaking. I heard Tom outside swear. I heard a thud and then the sound of breaking glass. I cried out again, thinking it was a broken window.

'This isn't going to be nice for you either!' I heard him shout. 'The longer it drags on, the worse it's going to get. It's a small village you know. Everyone'll hear about it.'

He paused and then I heard him walk slowly to the sitting room window. The dull shadow grew large on the floor. He must have been peering through the window again. 'We'll try and find something you know. If you won't settle… we'll have to find something ….' He trailed off.

I felt sick again. Dread squeezed my empty stomach. I started to sob, my mouth open and rigid in a silent cry. I let my teeth rest hard into my knees and dribble started to spread into my jeans.

He banged on the window panes, muffled thuds from the fleshy underside of his fists. 'Mrs Arundell. Please!' he shouted.

His cries made me curl up tighter, trying to shut him out. I don't think he said anything else and I heard a car start and pull away a few minutes later.

I came around slowly, becoming aware of where I was. I felt Jake appear, sitting beside me on the step. I lifted my head from my knees and wiped the tears and dribble from my face with the back of my hand. I sniffed noisily and looked away from Jake, staring at the wall of the stairwell. 'I'm sorry,' I said, gulping.

Jake didn't say anything.

I sat rigid, imagining what Tom and his solicitor might do next, what they might dig up. Nausea rose inside me, forced up again by the permanent clench in my stomach. I felt like I may pass out, drained by my constant state of anxiety

'I'm sorry,' I thought loudly to Jake. 'I can't go through with this.' He silently stood up and turned to walk up the stairs. Even Jake had a limit to his patience I imagined.

I went back downstairs to the phone by my desk. Cowardly, always a coward, I called Jake's mother at home, knowing she wouldn't be there.

The phone purred several times in my ear and then asked me to leave a message.

'Hi Margaret,' I said. My voice was shaky, breaking up. My throat felt sore, not used to the effort of speaking out loud. 'I've just seen Tom Riley.' I had to cough to clear my throat. 'I think we should settle.' Tears were filling my eyes and my mouth was beginning to strain with grief. 'I think it would be best if you, if we, settled with them.' I couldn't go on any further. I put the phone down, quickly enough so that it wouldn't have recorded the deep inhalation and the sobbing cry.

I slumped into my chair, tears running down my face, dreading having to face Jake's mother again.

3.

I wasn't Mrs Arundell. I realised Tom's mistake as I sat recovering. Tom had been presumptuous. Jake and I had never married. He'd never asked. I wondered whether he had ever intended proposing. Would I have said yes if he had?

I'd assumed he was married the first time we met. 'Hello. I'm Jake,' he said. We were walking in a group along the coastal path west of Plymouth. I'd joined a walking club a couple of years after leaving university, when the last of my college friends had moved away.

He strode up to me and confidently offered me his name as if I ought to become acquainted with it. I thought he introduced himself as a friend. His approach didn't feel loaded like the advances of younger men. It had put me at ease with him.

'Nice to see a new face,' he said. 'How did you find out about us?'

'Through the web site, although I had to ring up to find out when the trips were. It's a bit out of date.'

'Oh dear,' he laughed, a deep sound in his chest. 'I'm afraid that's my fault. Got one of the kids to put it up a couple of years ago. Not a clue how to update it.'

I thought he meant one of his own children.

'I could update it if you like, or replace it,' I offered. 'There are plenty of packages out there that will let you update pages very easily. Some blog or wiki type pages.'

He leaned closer as we walked along, raised his eyebrows and looked at me accusingly.

I laughed. 'Sorry. I could show you some examples of what I mean. I could send you some links if you've got an email address.'

'E, email?' he mocked.

I laughed again.

*

'So Lucy, what brings a young woman like you to Plymouth and our walking group?' he said later, as we walked on ahead.

I blinked, wondering at his drawing attention to me being a young woman. I turned around and looked at the rest of the group who were starting to straggle behind. There was a large proportion of grey heads above the red and blue waterproofs. There was a couple who were in their thirties, I guessed, and two large teenage boys, who walked awkwardly and scowled.

I turned to look at Jake. I wondered where his wife was. I didn't spot any obvious candidates in the group behind. He was middle-aged, his neck and face starting to crease with broken pink lines. I could see that some women may find him attractive, although I wasn't drawn to him in that way. I expected that his wife was similar - a pretty, middle-aged woman.

I smiled. 'I went to Exeter University, and just didn't want to leave afterwards. I love it down here,' I said looking out to the sea.

He followed my gaze and smiled too. 'Can't beat it can you. Been here all my life,' he said. I noticed the soft local accent in his voice. 'Haven't found a reason to leave yet,' he said, puffing out his chest as he put his hands into his trouser pockets.

I heard thudding and rustling approaching us from behind. A breaking annoyed voice said 'Sarge, Sarge'. One of the teenage boys appeared, sweating beside us. He frowned at me. He had a long scar through his eyebrow that made his face look threatening for his age. 'I thought I was gonna be leading the walk today,' he said, his annoyance directed at me.

Jake stopped and turned round. We were starting to leave the main group far behind.

'You're right lad,' he said jovially. He slapped his hand down on to the boy's shoulder. He was bigger than the teenager, surrounding him easily with his muscular arm. 'You go on ahead. Go on.' He patted him away.

The anger dissolved from the boy's face and he shuffled ahead of us.

'There's no need to worry about him,' Jake said looking at the boy when he had walked out of ear shot. 'Bit of a rough upbringing, but he's not a bad one I think. They're a couple of the kids from the police community group' he continued, looking towards the other teenager. 'I try and bring a couple along each trip. It was one of them that set up that web site for me.'

My mental image of Jake with his own children was erased.

'So you think you could sort another site out then?' he said.

'Yes, sure, wouldn't take very long at all. I can't do it next weekend. I'm moving into a flat. I haven't got much stuff but it'll probably take all weekend I'm afraid. But after that,' I shrugged.

'Would you like some help?' he said.

I didn't know what he meant. I didn't know if he was going to volunteer some of the teenagers, not something I felt confident enough to accept.

'I'm off next Saturday,' he said, 'if that's any use. Could use the van from the station as well if you didn't have something booked already.'

I didn't know what to say. Perhaps he wasn't married. I looked down at his hand but I couldn't see a ring.

'…in exchange for you helping with the web site,' he continued. 'My brawn for your brains,' he said smiling broadly.

*

I could see him from my bedroom window in the shared house. He was thinning a little on top. He stepped away from the front door and put his hands on his hips, waiting for me to answer the door.

He didn't look like I'd imagined. I expected him to wear a scruffy T-shirt, jeans and trainers to help me move, like the boys at college. He was wearing jeans, but he wore them with a striped shirt, woollen jumper and brogues.

I slid the window up. 'The door's open. Come on up.'

'Is this all you've got?' he said when he came into my room, looking at the neat pile of boxes.

I shrugged. 'Books, clothes, climbing gear, computer. What else would I need?'

He grinned. 'You are a rare girl.'

'I've just got to pack up a few last bits, but I'm pretty much ready,' I said.

'Right. I'll make a start with these then.' He leaned down to pick up an open box of books. 'I've got this one,' he said, standing up holding a copy of The Cuillin. 'Brilliant isn't it.'

'Have you been to Skye?' I asked.

'No, I'd love to though. I've always wanted to do the Cuillin Ridge. How about you?'

'Desperate to go,' I grinned. 'We had a trip planned at the university club but I got flu.'

'Well we should go,' he said.

I nodded enthusiastically, thinking he meant the whole walking club.

*

I stood with my foot holding the front door open on my new flat. Jake ran up the stairs, carrying a box.

'There you go,' he said.

I could smell his fresh perspiration when I drew close, our hands touching as I took the box from him.

'Sorry,' he said at the physical contact.

I shook my head.

He didn't apologise the next time and our hands seem to touch more with every exchange at the front door. At the end of the day he took my hand and held it while we drank a cup of tea, standing in my new kitchen.

I looked at his hand, pale and square with thick fingers, hiding mine in his large grip. I wondered if I could let this amiable man touch my body, if I could enjoy him holding my breasts.

4.

I was staring out of the window, the one that Tom Riley had peered into hours earlier. It was darker outside, the day looking like it might come to an end soon, its eyes half shut. I turned and looked for Jake up the stairs, but I couldn't feel him. I felt the weight of his disapproval though and I was restless in his absence. I stood up and circled uselessly in front of the empty fire.

I felt sick. I suppose that I was tired and stressed. I saw things sometimes when I got like this, when I was so tired that I imagined things moved when they didn't. I wished I could sleep. I almost turned up the stairs to go to bed, but I imagined Jake up there, keeping his distance as a punishment.

I looked outside again. I guessed there was an hour or so of light left, time enough to go for a run. If I ran hard for an hour, I would feel tired enough to sleep, despite Jake's disapproval.

I changed into my running clothes. They were in a pile on the floor in the kitchen. I was meant to have washed them and they were muddy and smelled of stale sweat. The tracksuit bottoms felt stiff and unpleasant as I pulled them on, and the sweatshirt smelled rancid as I pulled it past my face. I pushed my feet into a pair of running shoes on the mat and reached out to turn the key to unlock the front door.

It wouldn't turn. I stood, stunned, remembering that it was already unlocked. I stared at it, confused at why Tom had not forced his way into the house. A wave a fright rose in my chest. I doubted my memory for a moment. Had he stepped into the house? Had he stared at me, watched me as

I cowered on the stairs, lost in guilty memories. I felt disoriented, unsure at what had happened.

My hand shook as I removed the key from the door. I stepped outside, carefully, feeling the earth firm under my feet before taking another step. The cold air outside touched my face, sobering me. I shook my head trying to shake the memories back into their right place. How long had it been since Tom Riley had called? I looked around the trees and up the lane. There was no sign of anyone. There was no movement among the bare trees. I listened, but all I could hear was the rush of the sea down the valley and a crow somewhere above the trees. I locked the door and zipped the key into a pouch inside my tracksuit bottoms, and set off cautiously down the lane further into the valley.

The cover of the trees extended a hundred metres before I broke out into the clearing. The lane stopped in a round turning circle in front of the white Georgian house. It stood confidently looking out towards the sea with its eight square eyes. Nothing moved behind the windows, the house was dark and asleep. The stone steps up to the front door were patched with blooms of grey and orange lichen. The lawns and flower beds on either side of the path were jagged with knots of dead, dried-out weeds and long grass.

I stopped in front of the house out of habit. Jake and I used to walk this way often. He would always stop here, turning his back on the house to look down the valley towards the sea.

*

'I used to play here in the holidays when I was a kid,' he said pointing down the overgrown stream.

I shielded my eyes from a high sun and looked where he was pointing.

'We used to make rope ladders and hang them down the cliff at the bottom. You can't see it from here,' he said straining to look at where the valley ended in the sea, 'but there's a small cove at the end of the stream. Fantastic place to play.' He was starting to beam and glow with his recollections.

'There used to be a pool half way down there as well, beneath all that Gunnera.' He grinned pointing towards a huge rhubarb-like plant that had leaves an arm length across. 'I used to play hide-and-seek under there. And cowboys and Indians,' he laughed.

I tried to imagine him in shorts and a shirt running beneath the undergrowth, a bow and arrow raised and shouting without restraint. I could only picture a 40-year-old man running around with pale legs, long grey socks, one falling in creases half way down his leg.

'Did Emily and Lloyd live here at the time?' I asked. Jake had known the elderly neighbours well. I'd only had brief conversations with them when we moved in, but they had both died, Lloyd then Emily, shortly after. Jake had been the one to find Emily dead in the house.

Jake breathed out. 'Yes, they lived here for years. And Emily's mother before that I think.' He swallowed, a large bulge flowing up and down his throat.

'Used to be an immaculate garden,' he said frowning.

The sides of the valley, beneath the edges of the woods, were speckled with weeds, and patches of gorse blemished what I suppose were well-kept sloping lawns in the past.

'They used to have a collection of camellias I think, that everybody envied.'

I didn't know what plant he meant, but I was reluctant to ask. His eyes were glazed and beginning to water.

'I don't think Emily and Lloyd could keep up with it when they became frail,' he said, beginning to choke. His lower lip became uncontrolled and an un-masculine noise escaped his mouth.

I stared at him, perplexed by the broad, solid policemen breaking down. I'm afraid that it embarrassed me, seeing him shake and sob like that. It didn't seem natural and it was almost repellent seeing him taken over by emotion. I didn't step forward to comfort him. I didn't put my arms around him.

*

I shook my head to get rid of the uncomfortable memories and feelings. I looked down the valley. There was no sign of the pool today. It must have silted up and become overgrown with grass and weeds, and the Gunnera had died down for the winter. I tried to make out the path that followed the stream down towards the cove, but I couldn't see it.

I looked towards the house out of guilt, mentally apologising towards it for what I had felt, and jogged towards the trees on the other side of the valley.

A small trail led through the large beech trunks up the slope. You could see it clearly, cutting its way diagonally into the undergrowth, running up towards the coastal path around the top of the valley and towards the sea. I slowed my pace as I hit the first few steps of the slope, my legs tightening with the exertion. It was muddy today. Every few steps, my foot would slip as I forced my weight onto it, trying to push up the hill.

I was starting to sweat by the top. I felt cold in the breeze as I emerged onto the open fields and cliff tops. The wind was coming in across from the sea and was chilled and wet. The water was a rippled dark grey, mirroring the overcast sky above. I looked around. I could see for perhaps a mile along the coast, undulating green fields bitten into in huge mouthfuls by the sea, leaving the grey rocky wounds of the cliffs.

I followed the path with my eyes, along the bald green tops of the spurs, into the dips darker with gorse bush, past small exposed trees crooked and frozen in the prevailing wind.

The path looked clear, no-one out walking, only the odd white string of sheep following the trail in the distance. I waited, jogging on the spot, for a moment or two longer, looking along the coast and back along the valley towards Pennance. No-one appeared. I had the path safely to myself. I pushed forward into a run and tried to force myself to enjoy the freedom.

5.

I didn't see them until it was too late. I had been running for perhaps an hour and it was becoming difficult to see in the dusk. I ran quickly, carelessly, as I leapt and slid back down the path through the trees towards the valley bottom. I was almost back at the lane, about to break out from the cover of the trees, when I saw them.

The man was standing outside the front door of the manor house. He had his arms crossed and was looking into the house, his side turned in profile to me. He looked tense, his shoulders square and stiff beneath his jacket. The front door was open but he looked loathed to go inside.

A girl, just too young to be a teenager, stood beside him, also looking through the doorway. She held his arm, hooking her hand over the inside of his elbow. She twirled her long dark hair with her other hand, spiralling a thick strand around her finger. She bounced, perhaps trying to keep warm, turning her ankles out and snapping them straight again. She looked up at him and said something. Her question elicited a curt response that I couldn't hear. She stared back into the house, a look of displeasure crossing her face.

The man frowned and started talking into the doorway. I could see his lips pursing outwards, rapidly spitting out some words that I couldn't catch. He stepped to the side, swinging the girl out of the way, as a woman stepped out of the doorway.

The woman's expression remained blank as she passed the father and daughter, despite their accusing faces. She glided down the steps, placing her feet with the accuracy of a dancer, unhurried and in control. She had slim elegant arms that swung by her sides and her long cardigan made her look like she flowed down the pathway.

She had long dark hair, the sort that I envied, silky and shiny with hints of copper in sunlight, unlike my plain mousy hair. In fact she was the type of woman that I admired and envied. She must have been in her early forties. She looked pale, but not drawn, and she had a neat face. She looked comfortable with herself, a confident, elegant, grown-up woman.

She flicked her hair behind her ear when she reached the bottom of the steps and bent down to retrieve something from inside the car. I was expecting her to bring out a bag or a box or something like that, and was surprised when she stood up with a small child in her arms. I looked again at the father and daughter, taken aback that they had been ignoring the child in the car.

The child was around two or three, an armful of light curly hair and smiles for his mother. She stroked a few stray ringlets of hair away from his eyes and said a few words to him. He grinned at her in response. I was close enough now to hear him giggle.

'I can't hang around all afternoon,' the man said. He looked irritated and his lips curled around the words.

'Just get him in the house. He's not fragile, for God's sake.'

I didn't want to interrupt their family argument but I couldn't stop my progress down the slope and I stumbled out of the trees. I think I must have looked shocked, barging into their quarrel like that. I slowed to a walk, unable to avoid having to acknowledge them.

The woman looked up from her son and towards me. I would like to say she looked at me, but she did not focus on me fully, although she gave the impression of looking my way. She was beautiful, but she looked tired, distracted, her eyelids heavy across her eyes. She half-smiled at me, pulling in her lips at the side to communicate a wordless hello.

I strode forward in my practical efficient walk, heavy footed compared with her glide. She glanced down my body. I was covered with mud, my trainers heavy with a layer of soil spread thickly over the treads. No doubt I had dark sweat patches beneath my armpits and around my groin. There was plenty to disapprove of, but the woman maintained her half-smile as she watched me.

I put my hands on my hips, still breathing hard. I intended to wave and say a cheerful hello as I passed nearer, trying to act like I hadn't seen their disagreement. I glanced to the side, up towards the father and daughter. I'd started to raise my hand to wave, but I froze my movement when I saw their expressions. They were looking intently at me, directly into my eyes. They frowned, the father still holding his arms resolutely crossed in front of him. There was coldness in their expressions, the same look from both the father and daughter that made me feel uncomfortable. Their eyes did not leave me as I carried on walking and I twitched my gaze away from them, feeling too unnerved to attempt a greeting.

I felt sick as I passed beyond them, no longer able to see what they were doing. I wanted to turn around but was sure that they would be staring at me. I increased my pace up the slope towards the cottage, wanting to be rid of the family's presence. I could feel my back and neck tickle under the imagined gaze of their eyes. I tried to persuade myself that I was being paranoid. I spent so much time being anxious and agitated and guilty. I was aware of the effects it was having, how distrustful and irrational I could be. It was almost dark. I tried to rationalise that they could not see me. I was nearly at the cottage.

I stopped in the middle of the lane and reluctantly started to turn my head. My neck seemed to creak as I moved my head round, stiff with reticence.

I breathed out with surprise. I could see them all clearly. The woman held her arms wrapped around her son, and was turned my way. She could only have been looking at me. The father and daughter had moved down the path away from the house. They stood behind the woman but were clearly looking up the lane, following me with their disapproving glances.

I snapped my head around, my eyes wide and staring with shock. 'Jesus Christ,' I whispered desperately.

I walked quickly to the cottage. My hands shook as I tried to put the key in the lock, scraping numbly around the hole, missing the target like a child learning to play with an unfamiliar toy. I think I cried out with relief when the key finally slipped in and the door gave way.

6.

I stood in the sitting room bent over my knees, breathing heavily. I had started to chill in my damp clothes, the sweat cooling my back and the cold mud making my legs pimple. The panic was starting to recede.

My clothes felt disgusting though. They were still stiff in places with salty tide marks of old sweat. Damp greasy hair that had become loose straggled down my face. I stood up, wiping back the strands over my head. My skin felt clammy and dirty all over my body. I shuddered, uncomfortable in my layers of dirt.

I showered quickly, scrubbing my skin clean and raw, unwilling to spend too much time in a vulnerable naked state. I'd missed a text while I was in the shower. Jake's brother had sent a message: 'Calling in on way home. Be there in 5.'

I only had time to brush my hair and throw on a dressing gown before I heard a knock at the front door.

He dipped his head as he came in, taking off his black policeman's cap and slotting it under his arm. He ruffled his matted hair, short curling auburn locks like Jake's had been. The same large fingers and square nails scratched at his scalp. He reminded me painfully of Jake at times, especially when he was in uniform, that same hair and complexion, the same mannerisms and that deep voice with a hint of rural burr.

Ben was younger by several years though. He was not as tall or broad as Jake. Ben had large pretty eyes with long dark auburn eyelashes and larger fleshy lips, a softer more feminine version of Jake.

I could feel a rising lump of emotion in my chest when I saw him, the stress of the day releasing in the safety of his presence. I could feel my body wanting to run towards him, my chest and belly seeking to join the warmth of his. I wanted to hide beneath protective arms.

I had to concentrate to restrain my body, stop it from breaking down and seeking solace from Jake's good-natured brother. I had succumbed to him once; it must have been six months before. The thought of our warm naked touches followed by the chill I felt when he stopped to bring out a condom made me shudder. If I had never loved Jake adequately, I could never feel enough for his lesser brother.

*

'Hey,' he said quietly. He looked at me tentatively as he always did since that night.

'Hi,' I said as evenly as I could. 'Come in. Can I get you a drink or something?' I tried to remember how people acted when they received visitors.

He looked warily across the kitchen. He must have seen the saucepans still unwashed since his last visit. I saw him scan across the row of noodles and soups arranged by day across the kitchen surface. He could have said any number of things about the lack of nutrition, the obsession with having the same meals over and over again. He looked worried but didn't say anything.

'No, you're all right ta,' he said. He fidgeted with his cap, passing it from hand to hand, looking unsure as to what to say. 'Mum said you called,' he said looking apprehensive. It was almost a question.

I felt embarrassed about the message I'd blurted out to Margaret. 'I'm going to have a cup of tea anyway,' I said, avoiding the conversation. I went over to fill the kettle, indicating for Ben to sit down by the table. I left my back turned to him as I made the tea.

I watched the steam come from the kettle, a lazy plume at first, climbing and exploring higher in the air, turning into a jet, billowing with the scream from the kettle. I swallowed and cleared my throat.

'I want to drop the case,' I said turning around. I crossed my arms and held my breath waiting for his response.

He shuffled in his seat but he didn't say anything. He sighed, that was all.

'I don't want to have to go over the crash anymore,' I said. I felt tired and drained as I said it.

'But we're nearly there,' Ben said turning in his seat to face me. 'Mum says it could be over within three months.'

'Three months.' I paused wordlessly, my eyebrows raised, despairing at how long that sounded. 'I'm sick of having to tell the solicitors that the brakes failed. I can't stand having to go over it all, again and again. I don't think I could cope if we had to go through it in court.'

Ben looked up at me and leant his head to the side. 'It'd just be the one more time. Everyone thinks we're right. We'll get Tom for negligence all right, just you see.'

I gripped the dressing gown underneath my crossed arms. My whole body was tense. I started to panic at the idea of being under scrutiny for months more.

'I just can't do it.' I could feel my voice starting to break with the stress.

'But I thought it was what you wanted? Stop the garage from making more mistakes.' He looked up at me, imploring.

'It's what your mother wants,' I said coldly. She was the one who had started the case. Ben didn't have a reply and dropped his gaze.

I breathed in and out trying to stop myself from tearing up.

'Look, I just want it over. I want to stop worrying about bumping into Tom Riley and his friends.' And your mother, I added silently.

'Mum said Tom might have called round,' Ben said quietly.

A wave of irritation riled me. His tone was disbelieving, tentative at least. I'm sure that I had explained that Tom Riley had been round in the message. I had no doubt about it.

'Yes, he called round,' I said firmly. 'He made threats,' I wanted to add, but I didn't want Ben to enquire about how he could threaten me. 'He was very threatening,' I said less specifically instead. 'It was very unpleasant him turning up like that.'

Ben paused, looking as if he thought carefully before speaking. 'You can press charges for that you know,' he said. 'If he was here, and he made threats, you can get him charged with intimidation.'

The phrase 'if he was here' and the doubt in his voice made my irritation erupt again. I could feel my shoulders rise and curl with tension as I attempted to retain my composure and avoid an outburst. Tom Riley had been here, and he had certainly been intimidating. I remembered his dark unshaven face clearly at the window.

I looked at Ben. I could see what he thought of me in his face. I was being erratic, unstable.

'I'll leave it with you then,' he said sadly as he looked away. 'Let me know if you want to press charges.'

'You're getting new neighbours,' he said more brightly, looking up and smiling with the change of subject.

'New neighbours?' My surprise was that Ben knew about the neighbours not that I was getting them.

'Yeah, will make a change won't it. Not just you down this lonely old lane.' He looked pleased that he could bring me this information.

'Who are they?' I asked

'Karen Trevithik. As she was,' he added frowning. 'I don't know her married name. She and her two kids are moving back.'

I automatically turned to look out of the kitchen window towards the manor, but it was black outside. The sense of being stalked had returned to me again, remembering the family from earlier, glaring at me.

'Moving back?' I said, trying not to let my voice tremble.

'She's Emily and Lloyd's girl. You know the couple who lived there when you moved in.'

'Yes, I remember Emily and Lloyd.' I was confused. It was odd that the gentle elderly couple should have such an intimidating daughter, but then I clarified for myself, that it had been the man and girl who had looked unpleasant.

'I think I saw them,' I said, understating my concern. 'But there was a man with them. He seemed unfriendly.' I tried not to frown when I said it, but the effort only made my eyes water.

'That must have been David, her husband,' Ben shrugged. 'They've split up mind. I suppose he might have been dropping the kids off. That's why she's moving back here.'

'Oh,' I breathed out. I think my relief must have been visible. My shoulders dropped as the tension disappeared from them. I laughed, a reaction to the release of nerves, and self-consciously covered my mouth trying to hide my smile from Ben.

He looked at me alarmed. I suppose my laugh did not have a natural sound to it these days, it was used so little. The muscles felt stiff on my face as I continued to grin. It felt as if I was gritting my teeth, not smiling with pleasure. 'I'm sorry,' I said still laughing awkwardly. 'I passed them this afternoon. It's quite a relief to hear that I won't be seeing him too often.'

'What happened?' He frowned with genuine concern.

'Oh nothing,' I said quickly. I reached out and squeezed his shoulder through his thick coat, trying to reassure him that there was nothing to worry about. 'He just gave me such a horrible look when I ran past this afternoon. Made my stomach turn.' I looked away recalling the incident. 'But I suppose they were having a stressful time and weren't pleased to see me at that point.'

I looked back at Ben. His face had softened. He was smiling and his eyes looked wide and longingly at me, like a puppy. I withdrew my hand quickly from his shoulder. I couldn't help recoiling from him. I felt badly for him at the same time as being repelled by him. I wanted to apologise, but I couldn't explain to him.

We remained in silence, me recoiling and Ben looking pained. The guilt and anxiety began to descend again. I could feel Jake making his presence known. I thought I could see him leaning against the wall by the doorway to the sitting room, watching us. He didn't look disapproving. He was just looking out for his younger brother.

I straightened up. 'It's late. I want to get ready for bed,' I said flatly.

Ben looked confused for a moment, unable to keep track of or understand my changes of mood. He slid his chair back across the kitchen floor and stood up cautiously. 'OK. I'll make a move then,' he said looking warily at me.

He pulled on his cap and made his way to the door. He let himself out and turned to say goodbye. 'You'll have to talk to mum about the case you know,' he said, looking at me apologetically. 'It's not me you need to persuade.'

I nodded, looking down, pursing my lips together in acknowledgement.

*

I went to bed straight away, rushing around the house pulling out the plugs from sockets and checking and rechecking the smoke alarms. I switched off all of the lights to encourage Ben to stay away.

I couldn't sleep though. I lay on the bed, staring up towards where the ceiling would have been, the cold impenetrable darkness descending, kissing and stroking my face. My ears rang in the silence.

I was so tired. My head moved spinning and lurching with fatigue. I could have cried I so desperately wanted to sleep. I closed my eyelids watching the fireworks that my eyes imagined sparkling in front of me. The sparkling started to swirl in waves and made patterns for a moment.

I felt my head fall. I twitched and opened my eyes wide and gasped for breath. The air was cold and damp, shocking me awake again. I cried out, exasperated by my inability to stay asleep.

I cried until tears ran from the corners of my eyes, down my cheeks and poured, tickling into my ears. 'I miss you,' I said out loud, sniffing and wiping my eyes. 'I really do miss you,' I juddered. I coughed, choking on my tears, letting out uncontrolled sobs.

I felt Jake's cold presence. He lay on the bed, a clammy pillow of air beside me. I found it comforting. 'Thank you,' I said, wiping away my chilled tears.

Part 2
1.

I didn't speak to anyone for several days. I saw Karen drive past a couple of times, from the kitchen window first and when I looked out from the bedroom one afternoon. She didn't look towards the cottage. She was staring blankly forward, negotiating the lane, her slender fingers hooked over the steering wheel. I'm not sure if she realised the cottage was inhabited. I could forgive her for thinking its dark interior abandoned.

A large removal van came past, rattling the branches of the trees one day but, after that, there was no-one. I continued my routine in the quiet cottage, working, eating with moments of fractured sleep.

The next Monday I had to go into work. I couldn't avoid it any longer. I didn't mind the journey even when the weather was bad. It was an eight-mile cycle ride to the nearest station at Looe, where I chained up my bike, and an hour on the train to Plymouth. I liked the train, smooth and safe on its track. I stared out at the countryside. It would have been a pleasant commute if I didn't dread going into the office.

It was raining when the train arrived in Plymouth. Already sweating and wet from the cycle ride, I ran the half mile to the office, one of the new, brick boxes on the business park.

The front doors of the office obligingly slid apart to let me in from the rain. I jogged to a halt inside the reception area and took off my rucksack to find my pass. I could see the receptionist looking at me, considering me, pitying me.

'Awwww. Is it raining? What a shame,' the receptionist said peering over the counter, her eyebrows raised in the middle. Her voice sang its polite concern.

I didn't know what to say. I looked up at her and pulled a tight smile across my lips and carried on looking in my bag.

'Oh. Are you looking for your pass? It's all right. I know who you are. Just go on through,' she said, her head tilting. She smiled looking pleased with herself that she could do something for that poor woman.

I nodded my gratitude and walked past the reception desk into the main office. I pushed through the double doors quietly and made my way down the central aisle of the open-plan office. I stooped as I walked; hoping no-one would notice me.

My desk was in an area at the far end of the grey box, sectioned off with blue partitions. Only Peter, one of the other programmers, was in today. He had his mouth full with a chocolate biscuit when I dumped my rucksack down on the desk beside him. He looked up and raised his hand in acknowledgement and smiled with teeth full of chocolate and dark crumbs.

'Morning,' I said. I liked Peter. He never mentioned the accident. He'd never looked at me with that excruciating expression of sorrow. He just bought me biscuits when I looked like I needed them.

'Deborah was asking if you were in today,' he said apologetically.

I looked at him and nodded. I was hoping the new product manager was out today, on the road. I looked around, over the tops of the partitions, on the lookout for Deborah's long, bleached hair. She was in the opposite corner of the office talking animatedly to the development manager. She stood too close to him. She flicked her hair and leaned her head to the side looking up to him through her eyelashes.

I think I must have visibly shuddered.

'Do you want to do the peer review now, get it done, so you can go home?' Peter offered.

'If that's OK by you,' I said with obvious relief.

I unpacked my bags and sat down to prepare for the review, opening up the web pages on a large computer screen on my desk and the new code on another beside it for comparison. Peter rolled his chair next to mine and started scanning over the code.

'My two favourite developers!'

Peter twitched at the sound of Deborah from behind us. I heard the thud of her heels coming closer and rolled back from my desk and turned round. She stopped and stood over Peter, holding his shoulder. 'Hey guys. How's it going?'

She stood pushing her thigh against his shoulder for a moment as she squeezed her fingers into him. He blushed.

'Lucy, good to see you in the office for a change.'

She didn't leave space for me to respond.

'Have you seen the new admin tool Peter's finished?' she continued. 'Just brilliant. Finished it in half the time you estimated, didn't you Peter.' Deborah smiled down at him. He muttered something, his face contorting through several emotions.

'I have seen it yes,' I said 'It's very good.' I crossed my legs and tried to appear relaxed.

'I just want a few more tweaks,' she said smiling down at Peter. 'I'm sure you'll be able to fit them in by the end of the week.'

Peter didn't say anything. He nodded and coloured again.

'Has one of the developers estimated the remaining work?' I offered, trying to ask what Peter should have.

'No, I'm sure Peter will find them trivial though,' she said dismissively.

She looked towards the screen on my desk and frowned. 'Is this the new order form?' she said more business like. She let go of Peter and pulled up a chair. Peter quietly excused himself, picking up his coffee cup, and headed off in the direction of the kitchen.

I crossed my arms and watched her stare intently at the screen, her eyes flicking up, down and across my work.

'This logo's tiny,' she said pointing at the screen. She pressed her finger over the client's logo, leaving a smudged finger print.

I shrugged. 'Needed the page space so the whole form fitted onto the screen.'

'Surely we can reduce some of the sizes of the boxes to get a bit more room. Then our logo can be bigger as well,' she said smiling at me with her teeth but not her eyes.

I shook my head. 'They're too small as it is.'

'Rubbish, look at this one here,' she touched the screen again.

I shrugged again. 'I asked the client, pointing out that the header should be consistent through all of the pages, but he was clear this is what he wanted.'

'I know more about this Lucy,' she said emphatically. 'Design is my area.' I was confused at her persistence. 'But it's what the client wanted,' I said again.

'Change the logos,' she said loudly.

We both became aware of the silence of the rest of the office. No-one was talking. The tapping of fingers on keyboards stopped. She affected a laugh, throwing her head back.

'I'm going to let you have this one,' she said loudly and graciously. 'Go with what you've got there. Except....' She paused and rolled her chair closer to me. She put her hand on my knee and leaned forward, the top of her breasts squeezing up out of her shirt. 'I'd like to just tweak this bit,' she said leaning closer still, to point to the screen.

I turned and looked at her, incredulous. My mouth hung open slightly, speechless at the inappropriate tactics. Did she think that I would be swayed by the same flirtatious behaviour as the male programmers? Had she forgotten that I was a woman? I couldn't speak and stared at her uncomprehending.

She blinked and dipped her chin slightly. She removed her hand and rolled back her chair. She didn't blush or say anything about what she had done. 'OK,' she said quietly. 'We'll go with it exactly as you have it there.' And then she stood up and walked out of the section.

I looked around, looking for witnesses of her behaviour, but no-one was looking towards me and the background hum of the office had resumed.

2.

I had finished my review with Peter by lunchtime and caught the early afternoon train back to Looe. I enjoyed the journey back more, relaxing with the knowledge that I wouldn't see anyone from work for another fortnight.

It was well before sunset when I rode back to Pennance. I usually avoided the village when I cycled to and from work, but I was too tired that day to take the circuitous route home that avoided the descent into the village.

It felt odd taking the route, even though I had travelled that way several times since the accident. I felt uncomfortable turning down the familiar hill, entering the tunnel of trees that clenched tight around the road. It was darker under the roof of branches and the air felt oppressive although there were no leaves in the canopy. The air was moist and still and heavy. I felt my chest and stomach contract with claustrophobia and the nausea start to rise.

At the end of the stretch, I could see a hole of light through the trees before the road bent round to the right. I slowed, free-wheeling and braking as I approached it, staring at where our car had punched through the trees and undergrowth.

I stopped at the side of the road and reached out to a large tree. I ran my fingers along the edge of the thin green bark where the car had gouged it, tearing at its skin. The pale exposed wood underneath was still smeared with red paint. I looked beyond. Smaller saplings between the mature trees had been bent double or mown in half as the car flew through, spinning from the collision with the tree. I felt removed imagining the car from the outside; picturing its movement from the void it had left.

The wood was thin there. The trees only extended a few metres and I could see through to the pasture sloping down beyond the tree line. The field below still bore its scars. The brown cuts where the car had scraped and tumbled had started to heal. Grass was beginning to sooth around the gashes in the earth. At the bottom of the slope I could see the burnt sooty blemish where the car had come to its final rest. The blackened soil, from the intense heat, was taking longer to recover.

I felt vulnerable standing there. It felt as if something might happen to me if I stayed too long, tempting fate and inviting punishment. I turned around nervous that someone was there to deliver it. I didn't want anyone to see me and wonder why I looked so guilty. I heard a car somewhere behind me, out of sight, and pushed down on the pedals, eager to get away from the scene of the accident.

It was reassuring to leave the trees and feel the fresh air on my face. I raced down the hill into the village, letting the wheels turn as fast as the slope would let them. I could hear them getting faster, the rubber peeling away from the road and the air humming through the spokes. My eyes started to water with the searing air that ripped past my face. I saw Pennance get closer as a blur.

I squeezed the brakes as I approached the first houses and pulled them gradually tighter as I approached the green. I took one hand away from the handle bars when I had almost slowed the bike to a stand-still and wiped my eyes, soaking my fingers in a film of tears. I could see a blurred figure walking across the green as I approached. I paid no attention as I moved in a slow-motion cycle towards the side of the road waiting for my numb eyes to recover.

The figure approached quicker, becoming larger more quickly than I anticipated. I stared stupidly, directly at it, still unable to see clearly. I didn't register the blur of bright red on top of two trunks of blue moving to intercept me.

'Lucy.' The figure of Jake's mother came into focus in front of me.

She grabbed the handle bars of my bike, stopping my slow progress, forcing me to put my feet down onto the ground. She did not look as if she was going to let go.

'Lucy, well at last,' she said out of breath. 'I've been trying to speak to you for days. Did you get my messages? I left several on your phone and your mobile.' She looked at me accusingly. I'd unplugged the landline and let the battery of my mobile go flat. I hardly ever received any calls. Work emailed and so did my remote family.

'No matter like, you're here now. I'm on my lunch break. Do you want to come home for a cup of tea or a bite to eat?' She sounded friendly. Any one listening would have thought the invitation innocuous. I made a noise to indicate that I should get home and looked towards the road out to the sea.

'Well I'll talk to you here then,' she said more firmly. She still held the bike and dipped her head trying to catch my eyes.

'I've started a collection see, for Jake, at the post office. What do you reckon? I thought we could have some little memorial for him here in the village,' she said looking around the green. 'Perhaps a bench or something.'

I couldn't think of anything less suitable. I imagined the plaque on the back of the bench dedicated to Jake who never sat still and certainly never in the village. She didn't wait for me to offer an opinion.

'I've raised a few pounds already. People are so generous round here. Of course, everyone knew and loved him from the village. He was a very popular boy you know.' I did know. It was one of the things I had grown to dislike about Jake, how everyone knew him, and through him how everyone knew me. She was full of pride as she said it. She puffed out her large bulk of chest that hung low above her stomach.

'We might have a collection at the barn dance as well. You are coming aren't you, just before Christmas?'

I had no intention of going to the barn dance. I must have looked unwilling.

'Don't worry. Ben'll take you. You won't have to go by yourself. No need to worry about that.'

I wondered at her, how she was willing to offer me Ben so easily when she had never been enthusiastic about my relationship with Jake. How different her opinion was of her sons.

'We'll take good care of you,' she added.

I wanted to tell her that I didn't need taking care of, but I could have cried out with the need for someone to befriend me. I didn't want care from the Arundell family though, that is what I wanted to say.

'Now, something less fun I'm afraid.' She put her other hand on the handle bars and leant her weight on it, pinning my bike to the ground.

'Tom Riley's solicitor has been talking to Edward and he's come through with another offer.' She sighed, her eyes out of focus in thought for a moment.

I wanted to blurt out 'Take it, for God's sake, can't we just take it,' but I held my breath instead.

'I'm not accepting it.' She stood up straight, her chin slightly raised, defying me to disagree. I stared at her silently.

She flinched. 'But Edward would like to hear from you as well, because the case was started in your name.' She looked at me intently, waiting for a reaction. I nodded. I meant only that I understood what she said.

She cleared her throat. 'He also says that Tom Riley is sorry for calling round the other day, for giving you a surprise like that.' She looked up at me. She looked softer for a moment, her fleshy pale face perhaps looking sorry for the first time. She was an ugly woman. Broad forehead, square jaw, features that Jake had inherited more suitably as a man. I couldn't see any of Ben in her other than colouring.

'I've told Edward to direct everything to me, so that Tom shouldn't feel like he can hassle you. That's right isn't it.' She was standing up straight again but still didn't let go of my bike.

'Their solicitor is being a bit unpleasant about it, if you ask me. He said they'd have to rake over everything. Turn over every leaf again.' She was shaking her head, unintimidated by their threats. But then she didn't have anything to worry about.

I looked down at her fleshy hands, white with the pressure of holding the handle bars.

'But the likes of us have got nothing to hide have we,' she said pointedly. She bent her head down trying to catch my eye. She looked at me intently and I saw a look of perhaps disgust or hate quiver across her face, her lip twitching at the corner.

I felt sick. I swallowed trying to keep down the nauseous feeling and looked up. I tried to hold her gaze, attempting to look as if nothing was wrong, but my eyes watered from staring. I felt a cold tear spill over and run down my cheek.

Her expression flickered and she looked away.

'Anyway, nicer things… You're getting a new neighbour.' She stretched her swollen fingers and withdrew her hands at last. I had a strong urge to push down on the pedals and get away from her as quickly as I could.

I swallowed and looked up tentatively. She was looking proud of her knowledge. She widened her eyes and lifted her eyebrows to emphasise the appeal of the news. I didn't tell her that Ben had spoiled her announcement.

'Karen Trevithick? Emily and Lloyd's daughter?' she said

I nodded. I couldn't overcome the tension in my face to smile with any interest.

'It'll be lovely to have a Trevithick back in the manor. Known the family all my life,' she said proudly, crossing her arms and raising her weight on her toes and letting it back down again.

'Karen's grandfather was a famous doctor you know. An early psychiatrist or psychologist, or whatever they're called, but very impressive mind. Such a beautiful house as well. They used to have the poshest garden parties there in the summer. Very generous they were, Emily and Lloyd. Always thinking of the people of the village. And Karen quite the beauty when she was a girl. A wonderful family.'

I hoped that Margaret's association with the Trevithicks wouldn't taint my impression of my neighbour. I was starting to sicken at the mention of a Trevithick or Karen's name.

'Course it's a shame Karen moved away, especially with that husband of hers; never liked the look of him. Not suitable at all in my eyes. She could have done a lot better. But she'll be welcome back in the village,' she said magnanimously. She paused, and I wondered if I could leave. I twitched forward, thinking our conversation done.

'I've been around to see her already,' she said quickly. Disappointment sank in my chest at not yet being excused.

'She was busy unpacking and taking care of the kids. Running riot they were. So I only stayed two hours.'

I blushed, feeling sympathy for Karen and embarrassment for Margaret. Karen had not looked happy, quite melancholic. I suspected that the last thing she wanted was noisy over-familiar neighbours calling in on her. I wondered if she felt the pressure of being known as well, if she handled everyone's knowledge of her divorce with better grace than I would have done.

'Beautiful kids,' Margaret said. 'That Sophia is quite the young lady.'

I silently inclined to disagree.

3.

Jake was waiting for me when I got home. I was shaken by the encounter with his mother. I tried not to think about it too clearly. I didn't want Jake to hear.

She'd talked at me relentlessly. I'd often wondered how Jake took after his mother so little. I found her intrusive and I didn't know how Jake had turned out so placid and thoughtful. I imagined that his father must have been a beautiful person in many ways. I blushed, fearing that Jake heard me.

The first time I met her was when she invited us for tea and cake one Sunday afternoon. Ben had been there too that day. Her cottage was small but the two main rooms downstairs had been knocked through to make one large sitting room. She'd lived there since getting married to Jake's father and it was difficult to imagine how four such large people had managed to share the house with any comfort. Maybe that explained Jake and Ben's quiet, tolerant nature. It had been cultured out of necessity. There was only room in this house for one noisy person, everyone else having to accommodate her.

I sat on the sofa, feeling small on the large, floral suite bought for people of the large stature of the Arundell family. Jake and Ben were helping their mother in the kitchen next door. I could hear Margaret issuing instructions, Jake and Ben silently complying and clinking cups onto saucers and plates onto a tin tray.

I stared at the wall opposite. It was covered with a light beige wall paper with a raised flowered pattern that looked like it was made of polystyrene. I got up and went towards the wall. I touched the spongy white flowers, and ran my fingers along the stalks. I dug my nails into the stiff foam, testing what it was made of, and watched the dent heal as if it had not been touched at all.

A single painting hung in the middle of the wall above the fireplace. It was an idyllic rural scene, a hazy summer day of people collecting hay. They were piling a cart high with long golden grass. From a distance it had looked like the people were smiling and laughing as they worked.

As I stood close-up, the rough strokes of paint made the characters look harsher. Their faces were ugly and angular, their cheeks square with a single pale brown stroke. Their smiles looked more like grimaces and the darker strokes that shadowed their eyes made them look cross. I looked at the signature, a rough scrawl in dark paint. Eliza Trevithick, I think it said.

The door to the kitchen opened and Margaret led her family through. They looked taller when they stood together, their collective towering above me.

'Well sit down love,' Margaret said, as if offended. 'Make yourself at home.'

Jake smiled at me, a reassuring smile, and took me by the hand and led me back to the sofa. Ben and Margaret sat either side of the fire. They were dressed smartly. Jake had worn a pair of trousers from a suit with a striped shirt but had not gone as far as wearing a tie. He sat on the sofa, his long legs crossed. His tan brogues shone in the light, perfectly polished. Ben reflected the same look. Margaret wore a skirt and v-necked jumper with a large brooch attached to the side. She sat perched on the edge of her seat, her feet in kitten heels tucked back beneath the chair. They looked slightly absurd on her feet. A weeble on tiny heels that looked too fragile to carry the bulk of Margaret.

I felt underdressed in my jeans and fleece top. I had thick grey walking socks on my feet and had left my boots outside the front door. I drew my feet back to the bottom of the sofa, and squeezed my knees together feeling self-conscious.

'Well this is nice, having someone else for tea on a Sunday,' Margaret said, as she poured four cups of tea. 'My boys always come round Sundays,' she added, smiling at them proudly.

Jake jumped up from the sofa to pass around the cups of tea as she poured them. My cup rattled against its saucer as I took it from Jake. He smiled at me again and squeezed my knee as he sat down beside me.

'How often do you see your parents?' she asked. 'I suppose not very often if they're up in Scotland,' she answered herself. 'Fort William is such a long way isn't it. Never been myself mind. How long does it take in the car then? Must take a whole day. You must be constantly on the phone to them,' she said, half smiling and half grimacing at me.

She had paused at last. All three of them looked at me, expecting me to reply. I shrugged. 'I phone them every few weeks I suppose.'

'Every few weeks!' she said indignant. 'Every few weeks,' she laughed at my ludicrous answer. 'Your mother must be distraught not hearing from you for months at a time!' She looked at me, her eyes wide with disbelief.

I shrugged again. 'She doesn't seem to mind. She can always phone me if she needs to.' My parents had quite full lives. They had moved to Scotland when they had taken early retirement, and were trying to climb every Munro while they were still fit. We kept in contact more by email, usually them sending me pictures of the Highlands. They had been far too busy to worry inordinately about me.

The concept did not seem to meet Margaret's approval though. She looked at me, considering me for a few moments, her head drawn back so that her chin doubled.

'Well, I don't know how I'd cope. If my boys weren't in the same village, I think I would have to phone them every night, check they're all right. So don't you two go getting any ideas,' she said waving her finger at Ben and Jake. 'Every few weeks would not be enough for me, if you moved away,' she said pointedly at Jake only. She looked as if she had a tear in her eye. I wondered if it was real.

'Of course not mother,' Jake said affectionately. He squeezed my knee at the same time, catching her disapproval of my habits and trying to reassure me.

'What about your brother?' she said after recovering from her mortification. 'I bet he speaks with them more often. Jake says that he has a little one, so I bet his granny and granddad are in constant contact with them.' She smiled at the thought of such familial closeness.

I shrugged again. 'They see them more often I suppose.' My older brother lived in London with his wife and son. My parents took the sleeper train to see them sometimes, but they didn't talk any more frequently than I did. I didn't want to contradict Margaret though, and I let her enjoy her picture of my happy extended family.

*

Ben helped Margaret clear the crockery and accompanied her to the kitchen. Jake stayed on the sofa next to me. He was telling me about his father, how they played chess in the evenings when he was young. I was only half listening to him. I could hear Margaret's voice from the kitchen and caught snippets of her speech.

'Can't understand her family. Not right living so far away from each other,' I heard her say. It wasn't surprising hearing her say this behind my back. She'd said as much plainly to my face.

I turned and smiled at Jake, giving the impression of listening to his story. He was smiling, looking into the air in front of him while remembering his childhood.

'She didn't make much of an effort did she? You'd think someone serious would try a bit harder.' Another snippet made itself audible to me. I could only think she was referring to what I was wearing. I didn't mind her saying this either. I wouldn't have made much more of an effort if I had been forewarned. It seemed strange to me, dressing up among your own family, for tea and cake in your own home. I didn't have anything suitable to wear in any case.

Ben's quieter voice came through a bit later, in a pause in Jake's story. 'I know it's been a long time, but if he likes her then….' He trailed off. I pictured him shrugging. 'But I'm not surprised Jake has found someone,' he said clearly.

Jake had heard it too. He shuffled uncomfortably beside me, coughed and took up his story again with greater speed and volume.

'Really?' I heard her disbelief. She fell quiet for a few moments, perhaps getting used to the idea. 'Well I suppose it was about time,' she conceded, 'but she's just not what I was expecting. Not his type at all,' Margaret's opinion made itself plainly heard.

Jake held my hand for a moment and stood up from the sofa. He made it to the kitchen in two or three hasty strides to stifle their conversation.

'How's it going in here then?' he said in his policeman's voice. I could detect his controlled annoyance. 'Anything I can do to help?' he said.

4.

I was shaking. I hadn't eaten since breakfast and I had cycled over twenty miles since. I wasn't hungry though. The thought of food made my mouth water with nausea.

I went to bed early and tried to sleep, but I couldn't get comfortable. I was either too hot with the duvet over me or cold with sweat when I threw it off. The zeal with which Margaret pursued the case against Tom Riley made me anxious. The knot in my stomach had returned, straining painfully inside me. Perspiration burst on my forehead and back when I thought about the negligence case and Jake paced the house, uncomfortable at my guilty thoughts.

I got out of bed as soon as it was light. I had only slept a few minutes at a time during the night. I was still agitated, unable to settle. I had a sugary coffee and forced myself to eat some toast and butter. I had to eat it slowly, tiny mouthfuls at a time, otherwise I would have gagged.

Jake still paced around the house. I couldn't stand the tension. I felt like I might collapse with fatigue if I couldn't relax the grip inside me.

I flicked the computer out of hibernation and put on my headphones, intending to escape into work. I stared at the code that I had left open, but the words swam in front of me. I rubbed my eyes trying to focus on them, but the lines ran into each other seconds later, shifting eerily around the screen.

I stood up irritated. I couldn't stay in the house like this. But I couldn't go out to the village either. I didn't trust myself to meet Jake's mother again, not when I was as tired as this.

I looked at my running clothes that were drying stiff over the frame by the radiator. I was so exhausted, the thought of running almost made me cry. And I couldn't run along the coast anymore, now the manor was inhabited. They wouldn't want me jogging up their drive and through their garden.

I stood between the kitchen and living room, my hands pinching a fold of skin above my hips, not knowing what to do. A tear ran down my face, tickling my cheek, and dripped onto the floor. I jerked my head downwards, shocked by it. I stared at the splash it made on the quarry tile, watching it darken as it soaked in. I hadn't realised how worked up I was getting.

Without making a conscious decision, I put on my running clothes and walked out of the door. Even if I didn't have the energy to run, I needed to get out of that house.

*

I'd intended walking past the manor house without looking in. I was determined to walk myself sane again and did not want the sight of the family to discourage me. I marched down the lane, resolutely staring forwards, crunching over the gravel in front of the house. I couldn't stop myself though, couldn't help my eyes from straining into the corners, trying to spy the inhabitants.

It was a gloomy day, and the lights were on downstairs. I saw Karen through the window in the room left of the front door. She was talking to someone who was out of sight and shorter than her, one of her children I supposed. She hadn't seen me yet but I stood exposed, so that if she lifted her head she would clearly catch me.

I wiped away the tears from my eyes, sniffed to clear my nose, and turned to walk up the path towards the house. I had lifted my hand to press the bell when I heard voices muffled from inside. I could see movement through the moulded window in the middle of the door, small people spinning around in the bottom of a beer bottle.

'Why does George get the front room?' I heard a girl's voice shouting. 'It's bigger than mine. I should get it. I'm older than he is. I want to swap.'

A woman's voice, I assumed Karen's, replied more quietly, in a conciliatory tone. 'It's only because it's next to mine darling. I want to be able to hear him if he needs anything in the night.'

'What about me? What if I need something?' the girl's voice rose to a whine.

'You know you don't need me as much as George. Not while he's little.'

'You love George more than me. That's what it is. Everyone says so.'

'What?' Karen was quiet for a moment. I could picture her stunned and staring at her child. 'That's not true. Who on Earth would say...who says that?'

'It's obvious,' the girl said defiantly. 'I want to go home. I hate it here.'

'This is our home now sweetie. I know it's further away from school, but...'

'I want to go to dad's home then. Why can't I live there? Why can't I live with dad?'

'We've been over this. Your father has too,' Karen said patiently.

'Dad said I could live with him if I wanted to.'

This blow brought a silence. Karen did not make a noise.

'Well can I?' the girl insisted.

Karen sounded a little choked when she replied. 'You know that I want you and George to stay together.' She was imploring her.

'Why? I don't even like George. He's just a baby. I want to live in town and see my friends and live with dad.' The girl's voice became quieter, receding into the house.

'I, I don't know what to say. Sophia....Sophia!'

I stood frozen at the door not knowing whether to intrude or turn back. My hand was suspended, reaching for the door bell. My choice was made for me though. The door opened slowly in front of me and Karen's pale face looked out.

'I saw your shadow through the glass,' she said calmly. Her voice was clear without the door between us. It sounded clean. I couldn't hear any strong accent in her voice, some rural softness perhaps. It was lazy in delivery, rolling out across the space between us.

I blinked surprised at her several times. 'I'm sorry.' I mumbled. 'It sounds like a bad time to call. Please excuse me. I don't want to disturb you.' I started to turn round ready to leave.

'No, please, you don't need to go,' she said more quickly. 'It's just the usual. Nothing out of the ordinary.' She shook her head and smiled, her lips pursed together but the sides turned down, unhappy. Her eyelids hung heavily and she looked at the floor instead of directly at me. She looked tired and distracted.

'I was only going to ask if I could go walking and running this way. I live in the cottage,' I said pointing up the lane 'and I go out every couple of days, through the trees. But I didn't know if it was private. I've never seen any signs.'

'Oh no, you must,' she said stepping forward out of the doorway. 'It is a private road, but it's your road too. Please don't feel like you need to stay away. It's such a pretty walk up there isn't it? No, you must continue, please,' she tailed off, the outburst of enthusiasm draining her.

'Thank you,' I said. I stood staring at her. I'm not sure what I was waiting for. I was so used to people imposing their conversation on me that I was surprised that I could be excused so quickly.

'Would you like to come in?' she said, half raising her eyes so that she looked at me at chest height. 'Would you like a cup of tea?'

I cringed at my conversational skills and my hovering in her company. I shook my head, looking pained. 'Sorry, I wasn't waiting for you to invite me in. I'm sure you get enough uninvited guests.'

'I have had a few,' she said. She raised her eye brows lethargically in amused acknowledgement of a stream of villagers who must have called round. 'It's been nice that people have been so welcoming though,' she added. 'I'm Karen by the way,' she said, offering me her hand.

I was tempted to say that I knew her name, but I didn't want to make her feel uneasy, the way I would have been. 'Lucy,' I replied. I took her hand, wrapping mine around her slender fingers, not wanting to squeeze too hard. Her skin was soft and warm beneath mine. My hands felt coarse against the smoothness of hers. They looked darker in colour and drier from cycling and running in the cold. I withdrew them self-consciously and hid them in the side pockets of my running jacket.

'Would you like to come in?' she said. 'I'm inviting you. You're not intruding,' she said smiling.

I grinned after a couple of moments, realising that she was teasing me. 'No, thank you,' I said. 'I was going to try and jog along the coast. I'll get a stitch if I have a drink. But thank you again.'

'No problem. Be careful though,' she said frowning. 'That path gets dangerous in winter. It can crumble down the cliffs sometimes.'

'I'll keep a lookout,' I was going to say, but I became distracted. Over her shoulder I could see her daughter descending slowly down the stairs. I kept flicking my gaze between Karen's eyes and the large wooden steps that I could see dimly behind her.

Her daughter had Karen's graceful movement, pointing her toes down the steps, precisely placing her feet and letting down her weight in a controlled fluid movement. Karen's son was beside her. The daughter held his hand firmly, pulling him down the stairs with her. He stumbled down the steps next to her as if he was one of her toys.

She emerged from the shadows of the hallway beside Karen, standing straight, her chin lifted up.

'Hello. My name is Sophia.' She put out a straight, stiff arm in a strained imitation of Karen's adult movement.

Her precociousness left me dumb for a moment. I wasn't used to children. My brother had been several years older when I had been growing up and my nephew was younger than George. I did not know what behaviour to expect from the almost teenager.

'Hi,' I said, bemused. 'I'm Lucy'. I took her hand and squeezed it once.

I looked down at George. He had wriggled away from his sister and wound his way around his mother legs, clinging on to her trousers. He frowned, looking down, and gnawed at his shirt cuff. Karen put her hand down and ran her fingers through his curls. She appeared concerned and did not look up to meet my eyes.

'Do you live in the village like the other people?' Sophia asked confidently.

I looked from Sophia to Karen, unnerved by the daughter's dominance of the conversation. Karen looked reluctant to interrupt her.

'No,' I felt compelled to answer her. 'I live in the cottage up the lane.'

'The small, worker's cottage,' she said.

I didn't know whether to be amused or offended by her comment. 'That's right,' I said as plainly as I could.

She nodded, looking unwaveringly at me. 'So we are neighbours then,' she said. She smiled at me with a school-photo smile.

'Yes I suppose we are,' I said, strangely wishing to have the last word.

I stepped back, wanting to get away from their uneasy company together. 'I must get going. Sorry to keep you,' I said loudly as I backed away.

'Lovely to meet you,' Sophia said flatly, assuming I spoke to her.

'See you again,' I tried to say in Karen's direction, but she was still looking away.

I waved as I started to jog. Sophia waved back generously, her hand high above her head. When I turned round again, only Karen and George remained looking after me.

5.

My encounter with Karen and her family stayed with me as I jogged. It was refreshing to have something new to roll around my head. Thoughts of the accident, Jake and his family had dominated my thoughts for months.

Had she wanted me to come in? I was so unused to dealing with people. I couldn't distinguish between a genuine invitation and politeness that I should, in turn, politely reject. It was probably both I realised.

I think I must have jogged a couple of miles without being aware of the time or distance passing. I had replayed the meeting with Karen in my head several times, thoroughly over-analysing it.

Large drops of rain had begun to fall. They started to sober me and bring back my attention to my surroundings. I looked above me. I was under the edge of large dark clouds, building and billowing up the coastline from behind me. I stopped, realising that I was likely to get soaked whether I went on or turned back.

The large winter rain drops soaked my hair within minutes. I had to blink away the water that ran down from my saturated hair and into my eyes. Chilling streams ran down my neck. I ran faster as the sky darkened above me, threatening to thunder. I was sprinting by the time I reached the edge of the wood and the path down to the manor house. I leapt over the stile and started to slide down the path through the trees.

I was half way down, the white of the manor house becoming visible through the trees, when the right side of my body dropped painfully into the ground, jarring against my left; the two sides tearing against each other. I had plunged my leg into a hole in the ground, just large enough to take my foot. My shoe sank into the wet soil and became wedged beneath a tree root.

    I couldn't react in time, the momentum of my run carrying me forward and down the slope. The tree root clung to my foot as I fell forwards twisting my ankle and pulling my leg at my knee, straining the joint. I slapped onto the wood floor face first, the impact squeezing out my breath in a loud 'oof' noise.

    I lay winded, only able to take short painful breaths. I had fallen hard and felt sick with the impact. My stomach ached and my head swam. It felt heavy with the pressure of blood as I lay head first down the hill. I lifted my face from the muddy floor and spat out fragments of leaves and twigs, rolling my tongue in my mouth, tasting the earth with disgust. I was covered in mud. I could feel it cold and wet, seeping through my clothes on my belly and down my legs.

    I slowly knelt up, feeling dizzy if I moved too quickly. My ankle was sore. I could tell that it wouldn't take my full weight, but I didn't think it was broken. I stood up on my other leg, hopping on it until I could stand balanced and turned around to look at what I had stumbled over.

    I could see the hole clearly. I was confused why I hadn't seen it before. It was a couple of feet wide and about a foot deep becoming narrower at the bottom. I bent over, half hopping and crawling to look more closely. My head was still fuzzy and I stared down waiting for my vision to clear and the wood floor to come into focus.

    I didn't know what to think at first. I'd expected an animal's burrow, from perhaps a badger, but the hole was vertical rather than sloping into the ground. The sides were angular and regular in places. Slices of earth had been taken up by an implement like a spade. It had been deliberately dug.

I looked around the edges of the hole. A grid of thin twigs, branches and leaves had been disturbed by my fall, its criss-cross still intact on the edge. I realised that I hadn't seen it because it had been hidden. Had it been there on the way up and I had stepped over it? It was possible, but I had no way of knowing.

I tried to think why someone would dig and hide it in the middle of the path. Had someone built a kind of trap? I stared at it, feeling cold and sick, trying to think of a purpose for it.

My anxiety started to get the better of me. I looked around in panic. It was raining heavily still, large drops of water falling through the trees and tapping the earth and leaves below. I tried to listen above the background noise, half expecting to hear breaking branches with someone's approach. I spun my head round in all directions, looking out for dark human shapes moving between the trees. I was looking for Tom Riley. I imagined his silhouette in my mind and that was the shape that I searched for in my alarm.

I was breathing quickly, panting in distress. I got to my feet and started to limp and slide down the path, turning around every couple of steps, always expecting to see Tom Riley's dark face behind me. I thought that if I could make it to the manor house I would be safe. I repeated that belief to myself over and over as I lurched down the hill.

I could hardly believe it when I made it to the bottom of the wood, the manor house now safely within shouting distance. I turned around and looked back up the hill through the tree trunks. I couldn't see any movement, only the leaves on the wood floor, twitching under the impact of the rain drops. I felt less vulnerable knowing that Karen was a few metres away. Having someone living in the same lane made me feel less isolated.

I started to reassure myself. It had just been a hole in the path. I could have passed it several times. I couldn't believe that anyone could have meant any harm digging it, although I still couldn't think what it could be for. The worst that could happen was that I could sprain my ankle, which I had done. I felt the tension in my body start to fade as I talked myself down.

I limped in front of the house and up the lane, feeling easier, although I still turned around several times to check that no-one was there. The rain was falling heavier, in thick grey streaks through the valley. My clothes felt heavy and clung to my body as I limped home through the veils of water.

Jake was waiting by the front door when I stumbled into the cottage. I could feel him around my shoulders as I stood inside the doorway, dripping brown water onto the floor. I felt his cool arms around me. I was glad that he was no longer agitated.

Part 3
1.

I had a note from Karen in my hand, written on crisp white card. She had put it through the front door on November 5th, when I had been out shopping. I looked at the looping handwriting in black ink. It looked like a perfectly reasonable invitation, after I'd had time to let it settle in.

I hadn't been able to read it in full when I'd first received it. I had dropped it as soon as I understood its purpose, feeling sick at the idea. It was a brief note, written I'd guess when she found me out of the house.

'Would you like to come to the village bonfire night this evening? Or can we give you a lift if you were already planning on going (I don't think you have a car)? I will drop by at 7 if I don't hear from you. Karen.'

I'd turned off the lights in the cottage at half past six and hidden upstairs, sitting on the end of the bed, looking out of the window. I saw the branches of the trees outside illuminated in the headlights of Karen's car. I stood up by the window and watched her stop the car past the cottage. She got out and disappeared beneath me to knock on the door.

Sophia looked out of the rear window of the car, scowling. She looked up once at the bedroom window, her eyes looking straight at me but not focusing properly. I don't think she could have seen me.

I'd thought of writing a response to Karen afterwards, apologising and using the excuse of not receiving her note in time. I could have dropped it through the door while she took Sophia to school in the morning or retrieved her in the evening. I went as far as drafting a couple of notes, writing them out in my best hand-writing.

I became irritated with myself and threw the notes away. It was late morning and I had spent two hours trying to find the right words. Feeling nervous, I put on my boots and a fleece jacket and walked to the manor house.

I knew as soon as she answered the door that she must have been told of my background, had been made aware somehow of the inappropriateness of her note. She looked pained when she saw me.

I'd had my line ready in my head, practised and ready to say. 'I'm sorry I didn't receive your note in time'. I stood with my mouth open, unable to follow the script. She looked at me for a few moments. I felt awkward and she looked apologetic.

'I'm so sorry. I had no idea...' she started.

'Please, don't. You didn't know,' I blurted at the same time trying to stop her apology.

She looked like she was going to apologise again.

'Please,' I said, desperate not to talk about the accident. 'It was nice to be asked.' I felt shaky and fidgeted with the cuffs of my jacket, feeling uncomfortable at the proximity of a conversation about Jake and the memory of the accident.

She continued to hold my eyes with that half-focused look that she had and relaxed her concerned expression. She nodded her acquiescence, giving me a pained smile.

'Would you like to come in? Have a cup of tea?' she asked.

'Yes,' I said, trying to smile. 'That would be nice.'

I'd never been inside the house. I was unable to resist turning my head in every direction trying to take it in. I had only seen into the hallway and the stairs that clung to the wooden panels of the right wall. The hallway extended to the back of the house. Double doors at the end of the passageway, with a green glow through their windows, looked like they might lead to a garden behind the house.

'Have you not been inside the house before?' she asked.

'No.' I hesitated. 'I'd only lived here a couple of months when...' I shrugged hoping she would realise the rest without me having to say it out loud.

She nodded her understanding and smiled. 'They mentioned you, I remember now.'

I looked at her surprised. I'd only had pleasant but very brief conversations with her parents before they died. I didn't think they would have seen enough of me to have made an impression.

'They liked you,' she added sadly. 'They were looking forward to getting to know you.'

'I liked them too,' I said.

She recollected herself. 'Would you like a tour?'

I smiled and nodded and she guided me into the front room. It must have been a large sitting room I assumed from the sofa and chair shapes beneath white sheets. The walls were covered with a small-flower patterned wallpaper and paintings and sketches. The floor was hidden with boxes, some opened revealing piles of thick books.

'I haven't even thought about unpacking in here,' she said picking up a book from an open box. She flicked through it absently and placed it back on the pile.

'It's work stuff,' she said as an explanation. She hesitated. 'I'm taking some time off from teaching at the moment so I don't need it yet. I'm afraid this room is a bit of a dumping ground in the meantime.' She looked around the room languidly, as if troubled by it.

I cleared my throat. 'What do you teach?'

'History,' she said turning back to me, 'at the university in Plymouth.'

I nodded. She did not seem eager to talk about her work or her absence from it. The whole room troubled her. I wondered if it was the room her mother had died in, if Jake had found Emily on one of the sofas that lay hidden beneath the sheets.

'I'll show you the rest of the house,' she said, looking uncomfortable and eager to quit the room.

I led out and she closed the door behind us, turning a mortice key in the lock and leaving the key in the door.

I looked around at the other doors in the hallway. They all had old locks that had been painted smooth into the doors by several layers of paint. She saw me looking at them.

'Were you wondering why there are so many locks?' she asked.

'I was, yes,' I admitted. I imagined her having to carry an excessive key-ring, thick and heavy with keys to open every door in the house.

She hesitated, considering, before replying. 'They were fitted a long time ago. My grandmother was prone to depression you see, and was quite unstable at times. I'm afraid my grandfather added these locks so he could keep her in the room. It was to make sure she didn't come to any harm, to stop her from wandering off.' She looked at me and smiled at my reaction. 'Do you wish you hadn't asked?'

'Well yes,' I laughed. 'That wasn't what I was expecting the answer to be. I thought perhaps it had been a hotel at some point.'

After a pause, my response sinking in, she laughed as well. 'I should have probably have said something like that. It's not always worth telling the truth is it?' she said, half looking up at me.

'We live in here mainly,' she said standing by the door at the bottom of the stairs. The door was open but I couldn't see in. 'It's smaller than the front room,' she continued, 'but it's easier to keep warm.'

She hesitated again. 'I keep a stove running in here all day.'

My stomach automatically tightened at the thought of fire and I twitched involuntarily. I tried not to give away my fear but she would have seen it. She was warning me and checking my reaction after all.

It amused me, in a way, that we had so much pain, death and perhaps paranoia between us. She was loathed to go in the front room; I was adverse to the fire in the back. It was going to be a brief tour if every room held some ghost or phobia.

I stepped closer to the doorway so that I could see in. The stove was on the far wall, surrounded by a cage. It glowed inside, a red fire in an iron box. It made me feel nauseous and my throat constricted. I blinked several times staring at it, trying to get used to it. It was just a stove, I told myself, nothing more. The nausea would not recede though and I didn't think that I would be able to speak clearly. I made myself smile at her instead and stepped forward in a motion to show that I was happy to enter.

The air felt warm and pleasant on my face as I stepped through the doorway. I realised that I had been holding my shoulders high in tension as I relaxed them in the soothing warmth. It was darker inside but it looked more comfortable and informal than the front room. It contained an old leather sofa, with padded rounded arms, that had wrinkled and cracked with age. It faced the stove, looking like it sat in front of the fire for its own comfort. Her son was sitting on the rug in front of it, glowing orange in the light of the fire.

'Hey George,' Karen said softly. 'Lucy's come to see us.'

He looked up and stared at me. He was holding a small plastic dinosaur that looked like its tail had been thoroughly gnawed. It looked a favourite. Rejected toy cars, horses and farm animals were scattered around the rug.

I smiled at him and waved, not sure how to greet him. He stared for a few seconds longer but was uninterested and looked down again at his toy.

'I'm going to show her the garden. Do you want to come with us?' Karen asked him.

He immediately threw aside his previously engaging toy. He got up and ran between us, heading for the door. His legs kicked out sideways and uncontrolled, his feet thudding rapidly on the floor. I laughed at his spontaneous enthusiasm and Karen smiled at him with the first full smile I had seen from her.

Her eyes were focused and clear for the first time. She opened them completely, her eyelids no longer drooping heavily. They were a slate grey, glassy in the light that came through the doorway. She had a good smile, with white regular teeth and deep red lips. It lifted her cheeks making them look fuller, and pinched the corners of her eyes into soft creases. She looked pretty I thought.

'I think we have some company then,' she said laughing. 'Could you make sure he puts his wellies on? I need to switch off the soup,' she said going back along the corridor. 'He'll dash out in just his socks otherwise,' she shouted.

We were standing by the double doors at the back of the house. I looked down. George had his hand on the large glass pane of one of the doors, pushing it open.

'Wait a sec,' I said softly, putting my hand on his shoulder.

He looked up at me, surprised at the intervention, his mouth forming a small 'o'. I crouched down to his level. 'Your mum wants you to put these on.' I picked up a small red welly and leant it forward on the ground so that he could put his foot in. He looked at the welly and then blankly at me. I don't know if he didn't understand or whether he didn't put his wellies on like that and thought me an idiot.

'Can you put your own wellies on?' I asked.

He shook his head.

'Oh. OK then,' I said resigned.

I thought for a moment and lined up the two boots side by side. I held George under his arms, picked him up and started to lower him into the boots. It was harder than I imagined, swaying his small legs to line up with one boot and then the other without one of them being kicked over by George's wriggling. I tried three times.

'This isn't how your mum puts your wellies on is it?' I said slightly irritated.

'No,' said George, pleased with himself. He didn't offer any alternative.

'That's a great help', I said, and he giggled in response.

'Right,' I said with a new approach in mind. 'Come here.' I leant him over my shoulder, supported him with my hand under his bum, stood up and shoved his wellies on his dangling feet with my free hand. I held him at arms length to see if they had stuck. George looked a little stunned, but did have two boots firmly attached to his feet.

As soon as I put him on the floor he turned and dashed out of the door. I turned round to see if Karen was on her way back, but I could still hear her moving around the kitchen. I followed George out into the garden.

I was surprised by the size of it. I'd assumed the wood had surrounded the house and didn't realise there was a garden behind. It was a simple design, a few stone steps up from the house on to a large square lawn which was bordered by bare shrubs. There was a summer house at the far end, out of the shadow. The grass was spongy with moss by the house and I can't imagine it saw much light this time of year.

The main feature of the garden was a large tree, off centre in the lawn. It stuck out of the ground like a hand. I had no idea what sort it was, but it had an attractive shape, a short trunk and a globe of branches above it. George had run over to the tree trunk and was looking upwards, spinning around as he gazed.

I walked over slowly, so that I was within reach but not interfering with his play. He turned around and looked at me grinning, stumbling sideways, dizzy from his spinning. He pointed a small finger above him with an outstretched arm.

'Want to go in the tree,' he said grinning.

It was a good tree for climbing, plenty of low branches that curved gently upwards. They were still too high for George though. I wondered if his mother lifted him onto the lower branches and let him sit in the tree.

'Does your mum lift you up here?' I asked, patting the lowest branch at the level of my chest.

George looked at me for a moment or two and decided to nod.

I wasn't sure. I felt the branch. It was dusty with dry green algae, but not too slippery. I couldn't see the harm. I could keep hold of him while he sat. I lifted him up, keeping him facing towards me. He looked delighted. He looked around the garden taking in the view from this great height.

'Want to stand up,' he said putting his hands on the branch as if about to push himself up.

'No, you wait there,' I said firmly. 'You stay very still.'

I grabbed a branch and looped my leg over another, pulling myself quickly into the tree. I sat in the palm of the tree, letting my legs hang down the trunk and grabbed George with both hands to steady him.

'OK, now you can stand up,' I said.

He was very obedient and looked quite serious as he shuffled around and started to stand up. I pulled him up more than he stood in the end, but he still looked incredibly pleased with himself.

I saw Karen in the corner of my eye coming out of the house. She looked concerned for a moment as she cast her eye around the lawn. I had a sinking feeling in my chest when I saw her face like that. I wondered if I had overstepped my role and put George in too much danger.

I saw her turn our way, frowning, and then jolt to a stop as she caught sight of us. To my relief she smiled.

'Wait there!' she shouted. 'Don't move!'

She went back inside the house and returned a few moments later with a camera. She was still smiling as she walked towards us. I think she looked at both of us.

'Give me a big smile,' she said as she lifted the camera to her face.

2.

'He seems to love it here,' I said.

We were walking around the edge of the lawn following George who was dribbling a small silver football along the ground.

'Yes, he does,' she said smiling. She stood staring after him, as her smile waned and dropped from her face. 'We only used to have a small garden in Plymouth. David, my husband, wanted to sell this place when my parents died so we could move to a bigger place. But it's where I grew up, and my mother grew up. And I suppose I realised things were getting bad....' she trailed off.

'Your husband still lives in Plymouth?' I asked. I couldn't bring myself to refer to him as David. I'd had such an unpleasant feeling from him when I passed him that first time.

'Yes, in the same house. It's been a fairly simple split in that way,' she said plainly. 'I'm incredibly lucky that I could move out.' She looked around the garden and at the house. 'I think I'm going to love it here again, even though it's strange without my parents.'

'It's a fantastic place,' I said enthusiastically. I couldn't think of a more perfect home. I'd always loved the simplicity of its Georgian style and coveted its view down the valley towards the sea.

'It is isn't it,' she said looking half-pleased to find agreement and support. 'Sophia hasn't taken to it though,' she said frowning.

'Do you think she'll get used to it?' I asked politely. I would have been unconvinced if she had said yes, after the argument I had heard between them the other day.

'Perhaps,' she said. 'She misses her dad. And her friends.' She breathed in deeply. 'She hasn't been taking the split in general very well.' She paused and left her response hanging there. 'How about you? What about your family?' she asked.

'Mine?' I said blushing at the attention turning towards me. 'My brother, my parents, I don't see them very often,' I stuttered.

I wondered what else to say. I didn't know what else to say. I hadn't seen them since the summer. My parents had been in London visiting my brother, his wife and baby, and I'd bowed to pressure to join them and taken the train to visit them for the day. I thought it would be better than them visiting me, something they had repeatedly suggested since Jake's death.

I'd immediately wished I hadn't gone. My parents had opened the front door to my brother's house eager to see me. They couldn't hide their concern when they saw me: their faces dropping, their eyebrows raised, my mother's mouth turned down in grief. It had been at a low point for me. I must have been looking thinner and drawn.

I didn't know what to say about them. I had family and I worried them sick, shut them out? I looked up at Karen apologetically, sorry that I couldn't easily open up. She shook her head slightly and half smiled.

'I was going to have some lunch,' she said. 'Would you like to stay and have some with us?'

*

The kitchen was warm and steaming from the Minestrone soup that bubbled on the large range oven. The room smelled from the frying of the onions, garlic and bacon and the simmering of the rich tomato broth. I inhaled the vapours. I had forgotten how good the cooking of real food smelled. It filled my head, tickling pleasant memories, making me smile.

'That smells incredible,' I said without thinking.

Karen turned from the stove and smiled. 'Good,' she said. 'It's a favourite of mine. It's turning into a staple of ours at the moment.'

She gave the tall pan of soup a stir and started to cut some bread on the wooden side board. 'Please sit down,' she said without turning around. 'I won't be a second.'

I sat down next to George at the old, farmhouse table. It looked like it had always belonged to the house, the wood pale and grey with age, wearing injuries from knives and burn marks from pans. George scraped his dinosaur along its top adding his character to its.

Turning around in my chair I could see out of the window and down the valley towards the sea. It had turned misty again. The scenery changed every second that I looked, trees and shrubs coming in and out of view from behind clouds of vapour.

'I don't think anyone could get bored of that view,' I said turning round.

'I certainly never have,' Karen said, looking out across the top of my head. 'My bedroom's above this room and I used to sit for hours in the window seat, looking down the valley. Still do,' she said sadly.

She put the bread board and butter dish on the table and brought over three bowls of soup.

'Tuck in,' she said, sitting down on the other side of George. 'I need to cover this one with napkins first.' She started to try to wrap a tea-towel around George's chest, while George tried to attack his soup through her arms.

I gave the soup in front of me a stir, a pocket of its fragrant steam filling my nostrils. It looked so colourful, the thick red liquid suspending vivid green beans and orange carrots.

I took a large spoonful and blew on it, almost tasting its saltiness on my lips. I poured the warm liquid into my mouth and let it run down the sides of my tongue, eliciting a flood of saliva at the fresh flavours. The rich tangy tomato rolled across the top and the saltiness of the bacon rippled across the taste-buds around the tip and edges. The fresh herby vapours of basil and parsley infused my nose and the warmth of the tomato gravy seemed to fill my head. I closed my eyes as the warm feeling rose up my face.

It had been a long time since I had tasted food this fresh. My palate was so used to the one-dimensional flavour of packet noodles that it was overwhelmed with the saturated flavour of the home-made soup. I had forgotten what it was like to enjoy food. I had treated it as a fuel for over a year, taking it when I shook with fatigue, not allowing myself to indulge in anything so pleasurable.

I tried to swallow, but found that I couldn't. The back of my throat was constricted. My eyes had started to water. I covered my mouth with my hand, afraid that I might have to spit it out if I failed to force it down.

George and Karen had stopped their battle and looked up at me alarmed. My eyes were watering, tears starting to topple over and down my cheeks. I stood up quickly and turned around, hiding my face. I made myself swallow, the mouthful of food stretching the taut muscles in my throat painfully. I breathed out noisily, coughing and gasped for air. Tears were running freely down my cheeks. I couldn't turn back without them seeing my grief.

I heard Karen's chair scrape back across the floor and her footsteps around the table. I could feel her standing close to me, but she didn't say anything. She put her hand out, passing me a tissue, and gently touched me in the small of my back with her palm.

The simple, unfussy gesture made my chest clench with sorrow and forced out a loud sobbing sound. I snapped my mouth shut and held my breath trying to stopper my outburst. I gulped down the feelings and blinked my eyes trying to spread thin my tears.

'Sorry,' I said, sniffing and wiping my nose with the tissue. I coughed again, some of the soup having become stuck in my throat. 'Sorry,' I said again looking up at her, shy of meeting her eyes.

She looked at me plainly. Her face was not overwrought with false concern or pity. She didn't make me feel guilty at her attention.

I swallowed again, my throat starting to relax, and blew my nose. 'Thank you,' I said. 'I think I'm OK now.' I smiled a little to let her know that I was done.

She went back to the table and I turned around. 'Oh George,' I said concerned. I sat down quickly, and reached out to hold his small hand. He looked like he was about to cry, his bottom lip beginning to protrude and his head tilting down into his chest.

'Hey there. It's OK,' I said, smiling at him and still sniffing.

I wondered how many tears he'd seen, how many arguments he'd witnessed as his parents pushed each other apart. It must have been a confusing time for him, too young to comprehend the outbursts and changes around him.

'I just remembered something that made me sad,' I said quietly. 'But there's nothing wrong now, and nothing for you to be sad about. Everything's OK,' I squeezed his hand and he looked at me intently, frowning. I don't know if he understood, or if he didn't believe me.

I started to eat my soup, in small regular mouthfuls trying to show him that everything was fine, that I was all right. He frowned again, but reluctantly took up his spoon and returned his attention to his bowl of soup. Within a few mouthfuls his face had relaxed and he was pulling at doughy handfuls of bread and seemed to have forgotten any cause for grief.

'I'm sorry,' I said louder across the table to Karen. 'I'm not used to kids,' I shook my head and looked up at her. I was surprised to see her smiling. She didn't look troubled at all.

'I was actually thinking that you were quite good with him,' she said kindly.

*

I stayed for perhaps an hour after we had finished lunch, washing up the dishes and inspecting the toys George brought for us to approve. Karen did not look as if she wanted me to leave in any hurry, but I did not want to misread or take advantage of her politeness. I made the real excuse of having to work and headed towards the front door.

I stepped outside and turned around to say good bye. I wanted to say that I'd had a nice time but it seemed an odd thing to say. We were both such strained characters in different ways that it seemed odd to think us good company. But I did like her. She had enough pain of her own not to feel pity at mine, not to look sorry for me. I felt normal with her.

I stood looking at her, unable to tell her.

'Would you like to come for lunch again?' she asked.

I doubt she realised how happy she made me feel. I could have hugged her, I was so grateful that she hadn't found my company too awkward. 'Yes,' I said smiling. 'I work from home most days, so any day would suit me.'

'Come tomorrow if you like,' she said with ease.

I smiled all the way home, elated at the prospect of seeing them again, of their uncomplicated company. My smile only left my face when I got back to the cottage, its dampness closing around me as I stepped through the doorway. I shut the door behind me and listened out for Jake, the tension and chill returning to my stomach.

3.

I saw them every day for the rest of that week and the next. Whenever I left, Karen would invite me for lunch the next day. I started a routine to accommodate them, getting up quite late, going for a run and showering in time for lunch. I stayed for several hours some days, playing outside with George when it was dry, and sitting with them in front of the stove when the weather turned.

I would leave sometimes only when Karen had to pick up Sophia from school, and would work late into the night to catch up on work.

I started listening to the radio at home. I dusted off an old Roberts set that had come with the cottage. It must have been sitting gathering grease and dust on a top shelf in the kitchen for years. It still worked though, emitting a reassuring deep sound. Having started to socialise again with Karen, I found I missed the sound of people more. I put the radio on as soon as I came home from lunch and took it upstairs to let it talk me to sleep at night.

I didn't see Karen either weekend. I think she had her hands full when Sophia was home, or she was busy taking the children to her husband's house and seeing relatives in Plymouth.

I had to go into work the next Monday, so I hadn't seen them for three days when I called round the following Tuesday.

Karen looked tired when she opened the front door. 'I'm sorry, I'm running a bit late,' she said. 'Lunch will be a little while, I'm afraid. Do you have time to wait?'

I was about to reassure her and tell her not to worry, when I noticed George wrapped around her leg. He looked as if he would never let go and buried his head in the soft cotton folds of her trousers. I only noticed the deep red gash on his head when he turned to look at me. He looked afraid.

'Christ. What happened?' I said.

Karen looked pained at the question. She put her hand down to George's head, stroking gently through his long curls of hair. 'There was an accident this morning,' she said frowning. 'Sophia was in a terrible mood. We were arguing in the kitchen. George walked in at the wrong moment. She threw a cup in anger.' She paused and swallowed. 'She didn't mean it. It just caught George on the head when he ran in. I think it must have hit him with the rim. It was quite a deep cut.' She looked distant recollecting the incident.

'Is he OK?' I said feeling quite shocked.

'We had to go to the surgery to seal up the cut. It wouldn't stop bleeding. I think he's going to have a nasty bruise, but he seems OK other than that. I need to keep an eye on him today though,' she said, gently stroking away the curls from his forehead to examine the gash.

I felt sick, imagining the scene; his sister throwing cold, hard crockery at his fragile head, breaking the warm soft skin covering his skull. I looked at him feeling oddly protective, wanting to comfort him. He cowered away from anything that wasn't Karen though, unable to break physical contact with her.

I felt a surge of anger at Sophia. How could she be so selfish and careless around her brother? He was so small and vulnerable. She should be looking after him not venting her anger. Karen was trying to tell herself that it was an accident, but I could feel my face warm with rising anger. It was not my place to be annoyed though, to disapprove. I looked away and waited for my skin to cool and the adrenaline to dissipate.

I took a deep breath and turned to Karen. 'Can I do anything to help? Can I get lunch ready for you, while you sit with George?' I suggested.

She looked relieved, the last remnants of energy draining away from her. She looked up at me, at chest level as she often did, as if her eyelids were too heavy to lift her gaze to my eyes. 'Would you? That would be very kind.'

*

Neither of them ate much at lunch, only picking from the cheese, bread and salad that I put out. Karen stared at the table and held George on her knee while I ate a sandwich, too hungry from my run that morning to go without entirely.

Karen carried George to the lounge after lunch. By the time I had made the cups of tea and taken them through, he was asleep stretched across her lap on the sofa. She stared at the fire and absently thanked me for the tea that I put down on a side table next to her.

I sat beside them, turned slightly towards her, in case she wanted to talk. We sat in silence watching the orange flames lick at the window of the stove.

'Please don't think too badly of Sophia,' she said quietly after a while. She paused but I didn't interrupt her. I wasn't disposed to think well of Sophia from my impressions of her so far.

'She spent the weekend with her father and she finds it hard coming back here afterwards,' she said sympathetically.

'Didn't George go as well?' I said confused.

'No,' she said breathing out. 'David didn't want him this time.'

I sat rigid in surprise. Not understanding why George had not gone with his sister. I thought that Karen liked them to stay together as much as possible. I thought that her husband would be eager to see his son. She looked at me, and must have seen my confusion.

'He's never wanted George,' she said, no emotion on her face. She turned her head down to look at her sleeping son. 'I'm so grateful for him. It scares me to think I might not have had him.' She stroked down George's arm as she said it, and rearranged his clothes around him so that he wouldn't get cold. She looked at me again, perhaps wondering whether to tell me more.

'Sophia was a good age when I became pregnant again. She didn't need so much of our time any more. She spent time with her friends, and I think David had started to enjoy having some of his old life back again.

'He gets on very well with Sophia, they're incredibly alike at times, but he didn't enjoy bringing up a baby. It took over our lives entirely for several years. And at the end of it, I don't think we got on well enough to be able to go through it all again. He was right in that sense.

'He wanted me to get rid of George, wouldn't discuss it. David's a very determined person. Once he has an idea in his head he will see it through. It's very difficult to persuade him once he has an opinion on something.

'I'm not so strong' she said, unable to carry on for a moment.

'We even got as far as making the appointment for a termination and I went to the hospital. David didn't go with me and I had time to think while I waited. We hadn't talked about it at all. It was only David who didn't want him. I had been pleased as soon as I found out I was pregnant and wouldn't have thought about an abortion if David hadn't wanted it.

'I got as far as being dressed in a gown ready for surgery, he was so persuasive. Then I found myself taking off my gown, getting dressed and walking out of the hospital. I didn't tell any of the nurses. I was scared that they would stop me from leaving or telephone David.'

Her voice was even still, as if telling a story about someone else. She held George securely as she talked, as if protecting him.

'David was furious.' She swallowed awkwardly. 'He wasn't used to not having his own way. He made another appointment for me with the doctor. But I didn't go.

'We hardly spoke for weeks. I tried, but he is strong-willed. My mother came to classes with me for a while. I think it was only when his parents found out that I was pregnant that he was shamed into being more involved. I hoped once George had been born that we would go back to being normal. I thought that the baby would work its magic on him like newborns do.

'And he did soften a little.' She looked up nodding. 'But he did not want it to impact his life. It had been my decision to keep George, so I had to take care of him. That was his attitude. David wanted to carry on his life as before, going to play football at the weekends, going out with his friends after work.

She paused and took a deep breath. 'I could see his point of view in a way. It was a big decision that I took for both of us. Except that it was Sophia who lost out, not him. And I had been unprepared for that; I hadn't thought that part through.

'I was exhausted looking after George. I daren't let him wake David at night so I sat beside his cot, half sleeping so that I could catch him as soon as he started to cry. By the time I had taken care of him during the day, had done the shopping, prepared food for everyone, I didn't have any time or energy left for Sophia.

'She resented George. She learnt that from her father, copying his looks and comments that he made about me and the baby. They both hated me at times.'

I wanted to comfort her, console her, to contradict her accusation about the depth of their feelings towards her. But I had seen the way they looked at her that first day. Hate was not too strong a word for the feelings they betrayed.

'And the worst thing was that I was too tired to notice at times,' she said laughing with a sharp exhalation through her nose.

I was tempted to speak, to say that lots of families had the same issues when new children were born. My brother had been jealous of the attention I received when I was young, and we had a similar age difference to George and Sophia.

She shook her head though, stopping my protest. 'If it was only that, I think I would be able to make it up to her. I would spend time with her and try to explain how it had been, but she blames me entirely for the breakup and taking her away from her father, her school, her friends.... I don't feel like there is anything I can do now, and she is right, that is my fault.'

She paused and looked at me, guilty. 'I had an affair, that's why the marriage broke down and that's why I had to leave.' She turned away letting her confession sink in.

'David had already had at least one affair,' she continued. 'We slept in the same bed, but only because there was no room for any other arrangement. We were carrying on our separate lives, him going to work and seeing God knows who and me at home with George. I don't know how long that would have continued.

'But then my parents died. They died so quickly, within a few weeks of each other. It knocked me. First dad died unexpectedly. I'd hardly seen him since George was born and suddenly he was gone, and I'd never see him again. I tried to see mum more after the funeral, but I only managed once a week. George was catching every bug going around at the time and I kept making excuses. And then mum was gone. I'd missed my chance with her too. I felt very alone.'

I could almost feel her isolation as she told her story. I knew too well how easily a kind word or gesture would be too welcome at a time like that.

'I started seeing a colleague from work. I hadn't intended anything to happen. I'd worked with them for years. We were good friends and we had met up every few weeks, George permitting, since going on maternity leave from work. I didn't see anyone else at that time. I had no other adult company, so the first time we met up after my parents died, I just broke down. And I couldn't resist their comfort,' she said frowning with regret.

'It didn't last long,' she said, her voice heavy with guilt. 'Sophia was sent home ill from school one day. She should never have found us like that. I should never have let anything like that happen.'

She wasn't able to go on.

*

'She hates me,' Karen said blankly. 'And I can't blame her. She rants at me for taking me away from her father and breaking our family apart, and then she'll suddenly want my attention and need me to support her and love her. I don't know what I'm going to get when she comes down in the morning. It's worst after she's seen David. She doesn't want to leave once she's there.'

'Have you thought of letting her live with her dad?' I said cautiously.

'Yes, I have,' she said, almost embarrassed. 'But he doesn't want her, not full time, not yet, while he can't leave her at home by herself.'

'Does she know that?' I asked surprised at Sophia's attitude in spite of this.

Karen shook her head.

My stomach was in knots, empathising with Karen and feeling frustration at not being able to see a solution to her problem. All I could do was hold her hand in sympathy, feeling useless to comfort her, trying not to blurt out my thoughts about how horrible her situation was.

I didn't have the greatest amount of sympathy for Sophia, although I did not want Karen to see that. Whenever I looked at George's head, seeing the deep red slit on his forehead, my anger rose again. I didn't know how Karen remained so controlled.

4.

I kept turning over Karen's situation in my head that night, trying to think of some resolution. I felt badly for her. She had made very human mistakes. I thought her a well-meaning person, someone who should be allowed to be happy, despite perhaps making mistakes.

I found it difficult to empathise with Sophia completely, George was a soft target for her frustration, but I could appreciate how her parents' split would have been difficult and my opinion of her softened as Karen's story had time to settle. I involuntarily pictured the scene that she must have been exposed to, of Karen's affair. It made me feel uncomfortable and blush thinking of it. It must have been nauseating and hurtful for Sophia and I blinked and cringed, trying to remove the image from my mind.

Karen had not broken our habit and had invited me for lunch the next day. She was more relaxed, less raw that day. George had forgotten about the incident and was happy to let go of his mother again, and played with the favourite dinosaur on the kitchen table.

I watched Karen preparing lunch, trying to decide whether to voice an idea I'd had overnight. I had butterflies in my stomach and the words stuck in my chest, sitting heavy in a lump.

'I wondered,' I said clearing my throat. 'Would you like me to look after George one evening?' She turned to me, expressionless. I couldn't tell what she was thinking.

I continued. 'I thought you could spend some time with Sophia after school, perhaps go shopping, or to the cinema, or something.' I looked down at the table, starting to lose my confidence and wishing I hadn't started my suggestion. I hadn't thought properly what kind of impression Karen had of me, whether I was someone she would trust to leave her child with or whether she thought me the odd awkward, strung-out neighbour with too many phobias and hang ups, hardly an ideal baby-sitter.

'Would you?' she said surprised at my suggestion, reacting slowly to it.

I looked up at her. She was looking at me, almost focusing on my eyes. 'Yes,' I said 'of course. I thought it may help, you know….' I shrugged.

She sat down at the table, continuing to look at me. 'I think it's a great idea. Thank you for offering. It's very kind of you to think of it,' she said smiling. 'I did wonder if you would still be talking to me today, after my outpouring yesterday.' She looked ashamed.

'Of course I would be. You've done nothing wrong,' I said confused. And compared with me, I did think her behaviour little less than perfect. I blushed, feeling embarrassed at her gratitude, worried that she may think too highly of me and my generosity.

*

She took me up on my offer the next week. I called around for lunch as usual and then watched her leave, holding George's hand on the doorstep to wave goodbye to her. We watched her turn the car round, crunching on the gravel, and turn up the lane. It was quiet when she left, as we stood in the doorway looking down the valley.

I was scared, left alone responsible for him. I looked down at him to find him looking at me, perhaps thinking 'you haven't thought this through have you.'

It went more smoothly than I imagined, it turned out. We seemed to naturally continue our day together. We kicked a ball around the lawn outside the back for almost an hour. I inadvertently taught him a new swear word when I kicked the ball against the back door window. We sat in the tree. I read him three stories from thick cardboard books. He was tired by early evening and was fast asleep on the sofa by the time Karen came home.

I heard the car on the gravel outside and the front door click open. Karen came in first, eager to see George. She grinned as she came into the sitting room, seeing him safe and asleep.

'I'll put him to bed,' she said whispering, picking him up gently and carrying him grumbling half awake, half asleep out of the room.

I heard the clip of Sophia's shoes approach the door and stop, perhaps looking at her mother climbing the stairs. She appeared silently in the doorway as she stepped onto the carpet.

'Hi,' I said in a friendly way. I had been relaxed and sleepy from sitting next to the stove, listening to George's breathing.

'Hello again,' she said politely.

Her precociousness made me feel uneasy. I imagined her confidence came from her father, from what Karen had described. She had that comfort and belief in her own opinion that a confident adult might have, but she also had the lack of social restraint that children can entertain. The combination made me fear what she might say. I had grown used to George's behaviour, but I could not extrapolate that understanding to an older girl.

'Did you have a nice time?' I made an effort to say.

'Yes, thank you,' she said, politely again. She did not look like she was going to expand on their evening out and continued to look at me, comfortable with her position.

I wondered how long Karen was going to be. I did not like the prospect of being under Sophia's scrutiny for long. I looked towards the ceiling, trying to concentrate my hearing. I could hear George. He sounded awake and was babbling to his mother, so I got up and approached Sophia and the door.

'I should let you and your mum get on with your evening,' I said warmly as I passed and turned back. 'Will you let your mum know I've gone, say good night to her?' I said putting on my jacket.

'Of course,' she said smiling. 'Good night.' She held out her arm. I stared at her small hand for a moment, surprised by the friendly gesture. I took it and shook firmly, trying to hide my feeling of unease.

I smiled and turned, happy that the evening had been a success for them.

*

Karen hugged me when I called round the next morning. She wrapped her arms around my shoulders when she opened the front door, and squeezed her cheek against mine. It felt strange and soft next to my cool, numb skin. I blushed at the unexpected contact.

'I didn't get to say good bye to you last night,' she said letting me go. 'You were gone when I came down.'

'It sounded like you were going to be a while,' I said shaking my head and smiling, 'and I didn't want to take up your time with Sophia.'

'I was quite a long time,' she said still smiling. 'Come in, lunch is ready.'

'Did you have a nice time?' I asked, putting a couple of bags of food on the table to contribute to lunch.

'We did, thank you,' she said over her shoulder. 'We went shopping like you suggested. Should have known some retail therapy might have worked on her. I bought her lots of things in pink,' she said smiling as she turned round to put the bread on the table. 'I don't understand the obsession with pink. I never had it when I was younger,' she said standing looking bemused. 'I suppose I grew up a bit of country girl out here.

'And then we had fish and chips for supper. I'm not sure she liked that part as much. I suspect she chooses chips every day at school. I enjoyed it though,' she said laughing.

I found myself smiling as she talked about her evening. She looked the happiest I'd seen her. It was refreshing and I felt good that I had helped. It was nice to hear her talk unrestrained, chattering.

*

'I can see what Jake saw in you,' she said smiling.

She meant it kindly, but mentioning his name soaked me with a chilling feeling, down by body and legs, all the way to my feet. We were sitting on the bench in front of the summerhouse, watching George run around the lawn.

I was speechless for a few moments. I hardly ever thought of Jake when I came to the manor house. They were a break from my past and guilt. I felt like I had been hit over the head when she said his name, so unwelcome I found the reminder of him here.

I think she took my silence as disbelief or a need to clarify what she had said. She carried on fluidly. 'Apart from the obvious common interests: walking, outdoor things,' she said hastily. 'I can see why he went for you: you listen, you're considerate, pretty, good company. Complete opposite of his mother,' she said more quietly.

I had forgotten Margaret knew her, about how Margaret was proud of her association with the Trevithicks.

'Did you know him well?' I said still surprised, the words creaking out of my throat.

She thought for a moment, proceeding more slowly. 'When I was young, yes,' she said at last. 'We were at the same school, and I knew everyone in the village in those days.'

I think I must have stared at her, still perturbed at her mentioning the association.

'We didn't keep in touch when I left school though,' she added. 'I hadn't seen him for years.' She looked more cautious again, after seeing my reaction. 'He knew my parents better in the end I think.'

She stopped and looked at me. I could hardly speak.

'I'm sorry, I shouldn't have mentioned his name like that,' she said frowning. 'I'm being too exuberant today, thoughtless.'

It took me a while before I could respond. 'No, please don't stop talking. It just took me by surprise that's all. I should have realised that you knew him.' I drifted. 'Pennance is such a small place.'

I couldn't get rid of the cold feeling though. It hung about me for the rest of the afternoon. I felt disjointed. My skin didn't feel like my own, hanging strangely on my back. For the first time I wanted to leave their company early. I left before she had to pick up Sophia, making up a work deadline as my excuse.

5.

I couldn't work though. I couldn't sit still long enough. I paced the cottage agitated, unable to feel Jake anywhere. I sat on the end of the bed, willing him to appear, but he would not come.

I put the radio on loudly, hoping that the noise would talk over my rising fears, distract me from the nausea that clenched my stomach again. I went to bed early but I couldn't sleep. It was cold and I couldn't get comfortable. I turned over and over, thoughts tumbling around my head.

I stayed in bed until the usual time, trying to stick to my routine. I felt apprehensive when I got up. I think I was nervous of seeing Karen, now that I knew she was acquainted with Jake. I wondered if she knew him better than I did, like the rest of Pennance did.

I paced the cottage, anxious again. I hadn't realised how much I had relaxed over the last few weeks and how good Karen's company had been for me. I feared losing her. She was another person from whom I had taken Jake and I wasn't sure how to face her any more.

I tried to shut out those thoughts, wanting to be able to enjoy Karen's friendship a while longer. I forced myself into my routine, putting on my running clothes and trainers, and left the house.

It was a sunny day but cold. My breath billowed in clouds when I left the cottage. The first hard frost had left the sides of the lane glistening with crystals. The open valley in front of the manor house was white, sprinkled with ice. On another day I would have stopped to admire it with pleasure.

'Morning!' I heard Karen's voice shout. I snapped my head around to see her coming out of the front door. George trailed behind her, dressed in so many clothes his arms stuck out, his hands enclosed in colourful stripy gloves.

I reluctantly stopped my jogging and turned to meet her.

'Isn't it an amazing morning,' she said enthusiastically, grinning at the view. I nodded, catching my breath, my body not yet fully warmed.

'George and I are going to look down the valley before lunch. Do you want to come?' she asked smiling at me.

I didn't want to go. I wasn't sure if I wanted to see them at all that day. 'I didn't really dress for a walk,' I said, crossing my arms and squeezing my shoulders, starting to chill.

'That's OK,' she said, turning around. 'I'll grab you a coat.' She disappeared into the house and I jogged on the spot, trying to keep warm. I looked down at George. It was difficult not to smile at him, twirling around and jumping up and down, eager to explore the garden.

Karen came back with a large parka coat, throwing it around my shoulders, and hugging it around me. 'This'll keep you warm,' she said smiling widely.

We headed slowly down the path that followed the stream, George's short legs taking time to get over boulders and down the steps. We had plenty of time to look around at the changing view, looking back to see the house staring after us.

'I haven't been down here since before George was born,' Karen said enthusiastically. She grinned as she spun around taking in her surroundings. 'There used to be waves of daffodils here in the spring. I hope the bulbs have all survived. I don't think they've had any attention for years. Although I suppose things like that always look after themselves,' she carried on.

I shrugged and smiled. I didn't know anything about bulbs, shrubs, or any other garden things.

'Looks like Buddleia's taking over,' she said pointing to a grey-green leaved shrub with dead conical flowers. I looked around obediently, paying attention to what she said and where she pointed, wishing the excursion over.

'Wow, it's still here,' she said. She rushed ahead, jumping down a set of steps. I couldn't see what she referred to, and I strained my neck to see as I shuffled slowly behind George.

She was staring at a stone ring in the ground at the side of the stream. It looked as if the water should flow into it but the stream curled away and tumbled down the rocks below. The ring was surrounded by brown stumps and the net skeletons of large leaves.

'This was the pond my grandfather dug for my mother,' she said. She looked up with child-like enthusiasm. 'It's silted up now, but I'm sure I could clear it. Come and look at this Georgie,' she shouted, holding her hand out to encourage George towards her. 'You've got to see this place in summer Luce. When the Gunnera grows, it's just like a mini tropical forest.'

I started to feel sick. I remembered the same enthusiasm from Jake when he talked of this place. I pictured him again, a forty-year-old in school uniform running around the valley. I covered my mouth, trying to hide my sickened grimace.

'Shall we dig this out George? This summer?' she said, overjoyed at the suggestion.

I looked away from them, standing up straight and pretending to admire the view down the valley. I breathed in the cold air trying to quell my nausea and felt light-headed.

'Shall we go to the bottom?' Karen shouted up to me. 'You can almost get to the sea at the end of the stream.'

I swallowed, clearing my throat. 'Sounds good,' I said wincing.

Karen led the way down, impatient to explore the garden. George ran after her where the path flattened, excited by the energy from his mother. I hung behind, clasping the coat together at the front, trying to keep warm, wary of what reminder of Jake I might find next.

The path became shallower towards the end of the valley where it broadened into the cove. I expected to find the sea foaming at the end of it, but there was just a stony shallow pool. Karen and George stood at the edge, staring down. As I walked towards them, I could see that the sea was another three metres further down. The pool was hanging over the edge of a rocky cliff and the sand curved below. Karen held the back of George's jacket while she let him peer over the edge.

'Wow, look at this,' I think she said. She was facing away from me, towards the sea. She bent down and picked something long and wet from the floor. I thought it seaweed at first.

I joined them, and feigned curiosity at what she had found. 'I can't believe this is still here,' she said. She handed over the thick grey twine that she had pulled from the cliff top.

I gasped when I realised what it was. I think I gasped his name. It was the rope ladder that Jake had talked about, that he had made one summer. It felt cold and wet in my hand, water running out of the saturated strands and down my sleeves. It felt so real and repellent. I hadn't expected to find something so concrete from Jake's life, an artefact from his existence.

It felt as if I touched him, a cold dead part of him. He clung to my arm, touching me icily where the water ran. It wasn't like the Jake I imagined, light and ghostly around me at home. It felt like Jake was there, real and stony dead clinging to me. I dropped the rope, shocked by its solidity. I stepped away from the edge and stumbled backwards.

'Lucy?' Karen said with concern.

I looked up at her. She was carrying George away from the cliff edge, walking after me.

'Stay away from me,' I said. I think I was scared she would bring the rope with her.

'Jesus Lucy, are you OK? Sit down a second,' she said. She followed me up the bank, putting George down at my feet. I pushed myself backwards up the grassy slope, trying to push myself away from them.

'Luce,' she said, reaching out for me, trying to stop me. She grabbed my hand and knelt in front of me. 'Lucy,' she said looking into my eyes.

I saw her worried look, her eyebrows raised.

All I could say was 'Jake's'. It came out in a whisper.

Her face changed, her concern turning to sympathy. Her eager eyes softened as she thought she understood my behaviour. 'God, I'm so sorry Lucy. I didn't think. I didn't think it would affect you like this.'

She leaned closer towards me, as if reaching out to hold me. 'You poor....' she started to say.

I snarled at her. 'Don't pity me.'

She stopped her movement and sat back on her heels shocked at my outburst. It gave me space to start moving backwards again.

'Lucy wait, please,' she said, reaching out for my hand again.

I drew it away sharply. 'Leave me alone. I can't have your pity.'

She looked upset and confused, wouldn't stop trying to come after me. She kept trying to reach out and hold me, clasping my hand, holding my knee. She wouldn't stop.

'Lucy. You lost the man you loved. Why wouldn't I feel sympathy for you?' she clawed at me, desperately trying to hold me.

I shouted at her then. I shouted at her loudly and clearly so that she would stop and leave me alone. I shouted it as nastily as I could. I wanted her to be repelled. I wanted to extinguish her inappropriate sympathy completely.

'Because I didn't love him.' I shouted. 'If I did, I would have saved him. But I didn't, and I let him burn.'

6.

I remember the panic I'd felt when Jake's foot hit the floor, the brake not offering any resistance. Fright took over me, freezing me in my seat. I did not look at Jake but I could hear the terror in his voice.

'Shit. Shit!' he shouted.

I stared out of the windscreen, seeing the glowing trunks in the headlights blink past, the corner down the hill getting closer.

It was too sharp to make it without braking. We were going to crash into the trees whatever Jake did. I think he tried to aim for a gap, steering the car into the middle of the road, lining it up with the largest space through the trunks that lined the road.

'Come on,' he shouted at the car.

The engine screamed as Jake forced it down the gears desperately trying to lose our speed.

Then it took so long to reach the trees. I felt light in my seat, my stomach feeling empty. It seemed like we floated those last few yards. All we could do was watch as the trees approached and wait to see what happened. It felt like I had time when I remembered it, as if I could have calmly turned to Jake and seen him alive one last time. All I saw were his hands out of the corner of my eye, rigid and pale on the steering wheel.

The loud thud and crack of metal broke the reverie. The corner of the front bumper caught a tree. I was thrown forward, the safety belt cutting into my moving body, bruising my chest and punching my stomach. My neck whipped forward and back, my head banging on the head rest.

The car, caught by the tree, spun horizontally in the air. My head was shaken violently from side to side. I was a rag doll, my neck muscles far too weak to control my head. My face slammed into the door window.

The car hit a tree on the other side, whipping it in the other direction. I felt my throat constrict, as if someone had punched it, and my head was snapped back the other way.

The car landed on the ground at the edge of the wood, the boot and bumper hitting the ground first. The momentum of the rest of the car sent it into a roll. The noise was deafening as the car landed on its roof, with smashing glass and crumpling metal. I was showered by pieces of glass. I put my hands up, instinctively protecting my face, and something cold sliced at my arm. My head hit the roof of the car as it turned upside down, half my weight held by the seat belt, half falling into the ground, pressing my neck painfully into the roof. I couldn't breathe for a moment, with my head bent over and my throat strangled.

Then I felt light and air filled my lungs. The car was in the air again. I saw a flash of pale green out through the gap where the windscreen had been, the headlights of the car shining onto grass. They blacked out as the front of the car dove into the earth.

It killed the car's momentum. The car toppled over onto two wheels briefly and one last time onto its roof, sliding and spinning to its resting place.

I was upside down again, my weight on my shoulders and neck, my head pressed so painfully into the roof that I felt the pressure may explode through my nose and face. I could hardly breathe. My knees were in front of my face as I hung suspended. It was quiet. All I could hear was my stifled gasps. I could hardly see. The only light came from the dashboard and the glow of headlights outside, shining into the dark air.

My face was wet and cool. I worried at first that I might be covered in blood, but my shallow breaths started to catch the aromatic fumes. I could taste the paraffin on my lips and I started to panic.

The bottle of paraffin for Jake's old camping stove must have burst. I was covered in it. I clenched my hands. They were wet. All I could breathe were its vapours as it spread and started to evaporate, making a flammable pocket of gas in the car.

I made a noise at the back of my throat, a strangled cry and moan. I tried to turn my head to see Jake, crunching my scalp in broken glass as I turned. I tried to say his name but my throat was too tightly folded.

There was no movement from his side of the car. I could only just make out his shape. He was more contorted against the roof than I was. His arms lay limp by his sides, one resting on my shoulder. I tried to squeeze it, but I couldn't bend my hand back far enough. The movement nudged his arm from me and it fell with a heavy thud on the roof.

I did not stop to check his pulse. I didn't squirm so that I could say his name. In my panic, I was glad that he was dead, so that I didn't need to stop and help him. I was overwhelmed by the urge to save my own life with no more than this cursory consideration of his.

I started grabbing above me trying to find the seat belt release. My arm that had been nearest the window wouldn't work properly. I couldn't curl my fingers round with any strength. I didn't wonder why. I shuffled and squirmed more on my shoulders, trying to give my other arm room to reach the safety belt.

    My knees dropped and hit my face as I released the catch. I kicked them out and started to thrash and squirm, trying to turn my body to slide out of the broken window of the side door.

    The gap was small and crumpled. I could only squeeze my head out if I turned it sideways. I grabbed at the edge of the door with my hands, trying to pull my body through. My arm sent blinding waves of pain through my head. I think I was crying out loudly.

    I kicked my legs trying to push myself through. My feet pounded something soft as I tried to scramble out. I realised afterwards, when I retold my story, that it would have been Jake that I kicked and beat.

    My back was stuck on something sharp, a jagged edge where the roof had creased. My back hurt when I pushed, the fold of metal scraping down my skin, and it dug in painfully when I stopped. I was starting to cry in helplessness, starting to despair, when I smelled burning. I don't know where it was coming from but my body tensed in desperation and I started kicking wildly to squeeze myself through the window. The movement tore down my back as I squeezed through.

    I rolled over onto my knees and crawled with one arm desperately across the grass. I was weak, and my arm gave way, my face thumping into the ground. I turned over and looked back to see if I was far enough away, crying with every breath.

The inside of the car lit up in an instant, the flames rushing out in a howl. All I could see was fire for a moment, a glowing ball in front of me, before the flames were dragged back inside the car to feast on the interior. I saw Jake's dark body. I saw his crumpled form being licked by the orange and yellow. And then I saw him move.

It was just a single movement, but unmistakably a movement. He had lifted his head, his neck and chest tensing up with the effort. I could see his mouth open, the gaping space his lips made silhouetted against the glow. His chest collapsed and his head rolled to the side. I stared at his blackening shape, my mouth open but no longer able to cry or scream. I stared at him, seeing his agonised shape flicker between the flames. I watched him burn, blister and disintegrate.

*

Someone dragged me back further away from the car, but I couldn't take my eyes from Jake's burning corpse. I could hear a man and woman's voice around me, but didn't hear what they said. I only blinked when the dark shape of someone crouching in front of me blocked out the orange glow. Someone told me later that it was the driver from the car we had passed coming the other way. I wouldn't recognise him now. I'm not sure if I looked at his face then.

'What happened?' he asked.

I told him, reliving it in detail, everything except that I had seen Jake move and witnessed his silent, arid cry. I couldn't speak when I came to that part. And everyone took it that I was too overwhelmed to talk about it: the man who dragged me away from the car, his wife, the policeman, the fireman, the solicitor, Ben, Margaret, my parents, my brother. Over and over I had to tell my story, until there was no possibility that it could ever fade in my memory.

*

I hardly had to think to recount my story to Karen. I recited it, told her everything, while I stared not caring what she thought anymore. She had followed me home. It was strange and sobering seeing her in the cottage. I sat on the sofa, staring at the empty fireplace looking over her shoulder as she knelt in front of me. She held my hands, listening intently, her concerned eyes never leaving mine.

I couldn't feel anything anymore, I could no longer cry and she was too shocked to say anything.

7.

She asked me all the same questions I had asked myself. Would I have been able to save him, without being caught in the fire? Could I have pulled a full grown man from the car when I had trouble moving? I think she realised that the answer to these questions could not ease my guilt. She did not push her questions, did not patronise me by saying I was being unfair to myself. She looked troubled by my state and agitated perhaps that she could not help.

She didn't ask the question that troubled me most, however; the question that I hardly ever dared ask myself.

I had never loved Jake in a romantic way. Not in the way that makes your chest ache when you're apart or makes you high when you're together. I had felt that for a while with boys at college. I think they were typical young relationships; hormonal, argumentative, intense. I could never have lived with any of them though.

I'd worried, that time Jake helped me move, whether I could find him appealing enough to physically love him. I wondered if I was stringing him along, taking advantage of his generosity. He knew I did not find him attractive. He was experienced enough to recognise that that insatiable longing was absent. So he took things slowly, considerately, and I found that I could let him enjoy me.

We'd got on incredibly well when we moved in together. Through the guilt I felt at his death and all the pain, it was easy to forget how well we lived together. It was easy. It wasn't only that we liked the same hobbies, had the same tastes in food and television programmes. It was the way we did things. If we cooked a meal, we would move fluidly around the kitchen, around each other, attending to whatever needed doing next, neither of us taking the lead.

It was when we moved into the cottage that we had our first and I think only argument. It wasn't even a proper argument. Neither of us raised our voices. I was handing boxes up to Jake through the loft hatch. He seemed to have twice the amount of belongings compared with me. I suppose my school books and things from university were still stored at my parents', whereas Jake had everything he owned. They were mostly plain, neat, grey cardboard boxes labelled 'LPs', 'old course books', all permanently sealed with wide strips of brown tape, except for a smaller red shoe box. It wasn't sealed and the lid was loose. It fell open when I picked it up.

'Hey, are these old photos of you?' I asked, excited by the glimpse of a younger Jake at the top of the box. It was a faded colour photo of him walking in mountains, somewhere with bigger proportions than England, perhaps the Alps. I was amused by his hair which was longer than I was used to seeing it, springing out in a ginger afro. I started to flick through the pile of photos, smiling at what I might find.

'Oi! Hand those over,' he said.

'Just a minute,' I said laughing, continuing to walk my fingers through the pile.

'I'm serious,' I heard him say sternly.

I looked up at him surprised. It was the firmest he had ever been with me. I could see his face clearly looking down at me, leaning down on all fours with his fingers curled around the edges of the loft hatch. He didn't look cross, just determined.

I acquiesced. 'OK,' I said, letting him hear my surprise but not disobeying him. I put the lid back on the box. I stepped up a couple of rungs on the ladder and handed up the container.

He leant down through the loft hatch and kissed me on the forehead. 'Thank you,' he said. 'There's nothing for you to worry about in there, it's just, well personal I suppose.'

I did know what he meant. There were things about my life that I wouldn't want to tell him or show him. I didn't worry that they would alter his opinion of me, but I didn't want to go through the discomfort of remembering and telling him those stories; a secret crush on a teacher, an intimate encounter with a friend, normal uncomfortable things. We carried on moving the boxes into the loft and didn't speak about it again.

I saw that box every time I went in the loft. I could see the side of it in the wedge of light when I opened the hatch, tempting me. Jake had been on nights one time, not long before the accident, when I was putting some old books up out of the way. I had all evening to myself, and I couldn't resist sliding over the box and peaking inside, and then taking it downstairs to look at it properly.

It was mainly photos like I had remembered, with the odd object: a prefect badge, a graffitied pencil tin. I flicked through them again cautiously. I found a school portrait of Jake with Ben. Jake must have been in the sixth form, almost a full grown man, with Ben still a child sitting next to him. They both had vivid ginger hair, the swirling blue background bringing out all their freckles.

Near the bottom I found another mounted photo. It was of a small group of people in black tie with silver italic writing on the card border: a policeman's ball. Jake did not look much older than in his school portrait. He couldn't have been in the force for very long.

He was in the front of the group, next to a girl, a young woman. She looked pretty, wearing a long silky dress, holding herself in a feminine pose that I could never manage without feeling self-conscious. Her slim arms hung by her sides, with elegant ease.

The way Jake stood next to her made my heart stumble and my stomach freeze. He held her hand in both of his, clinging on to her, protecting her. He looked at her with an expression on his face that I had never seen from him. His eyes were wide and keen. His face was flushed. He inclined his head towards the girl. He adored her.

I blushed at what I'd seen. I'd had a glimpse of him that I shouldn't have. I felt as guilty sitting there as if he had been in the room watching me. I dropped the pile of photos back into the box and quickly covered it with the lid. I rushed up the stairs and up into the loft to put it back, shaking as I pushed it into the darkness.

He had been in love with that girl. And now that I knew what Jake in love looked like, I realised that he had settled for me, agreeable, sporty Lucy with all the same hobbies.

And that was what made me feel most sick with guilt, not that I might have left him in the car to die because I didn't love him, but because he didn't love me.

Part 4
1.

My admission to Karen was both terrifying and a relief. It gave me a nervous energy, thinking how much I had trusted her. She had taken my admission better than I could have hoped for. She only had consoling words for me. But I know how things can change after they are left to sink in and fester.

I hardly saw her over the next few days. Sophia was home with flu at the beginning of the week and then Karen had a friend round on the Friday. She phoned me before she went to bed though, just to check I was all right and to say good night. And then she would text in the morning to say hello. It was comforting to hear her voice last thing at night and to be thought of first thing.

It made me more lonely and restless, having those tantalising snippets of her company. I was desperate to get out of the cottage. Apart from going out running I hadn't left it for several days.

When Ben phoned at the weekend to ask one last time about accompanying him to the barn dance, I surprised him by saying yes. It was only a partial acceptance. I agreed to meet him at the pub by Pennance green beforehand, for a drink only.

The front room of the pub was full. The young farmers were out in numbers, starting their drinking early. I had to push my arm through, in between humid backs, levering bodies gently apart to get past. Ben was already there, leaning on the bar, holding a pint of bitter and talking to the landlord.

'Hey,' I said, as I squeezed myself next to him.

I'd taken him by surprise, appearing behind him and then sliding my way around to the bar. He looked at me worried when he found himself in close contact with me. I smiled at him, trying to put him at ease.

'Can I get you a drink,' he stuttered, staring at me with wide eyes.

'Why not?' I said trying to sound relaxed. 'Well a half anyway.'

He repeated my order to the landlord, and stared after him, occasionally flicking his gaze down to me. I'd worn my hair down that evening. I'd become sick of the sight of myself while getting ready to come out, the same sad plain face with hair drawn back tight. I'd brushed my hair out and long. It wasn't in too bad a state considering I hadn't had it cut for over a year. I'd even put on a small amount of eyeliner and mascara. It had been strange seeing my familiar face in the mirror. It was like seeing an old photograph of me.

'Still can't tempt you to come out after?' Ben said. 'Looks like it's going to be popular.' He looked around the bar indicating the enthusiastic crowd.

'Not my thing,' I said wrinkling my nose and smiling. I took a sip from my drink and then looked up at him to say something. He was staring at someone over the top of my head. I tried to turn around to see what he was looking at.

'Can I get you anything to eat? Crisps or anything?' he said distracting me.

I laughed, amused at him trying to find desperate things to say. Was I that uncomfortable company, I wondered. 'No thanks,' I said smiling at him.

I heard a voice from further along the bar over the hum of the crowd; a man's voice, slurring and irritated. I felt a shiver of fear as I recognised the voice. It was the growl of Tom Riley.

'I just want another pint,' he said, his tongue numb over the 't's. I couldn't hear what the landlord said, but I could see him on the other side of the bar, his arms crossed in front of him, looking uncooperative.

'Just give me another fucking drink,' Tom Riley shouted.

I flinched at his voice, feeling vulnerable so close to him. I feared encountering him when sober, I was terrified of what he might do when he was drunk and out of control. I started to feel claustrophobic, trapped by warm bodies at the bar. I looked over my shoulder though gaps in the heads of the crowd and saw his dark greasy hair just a couple of metres away.

He was leaning on the bar with his arms outstretched, supporting himself while trying to look authoritative. He looked worse than when I had seen him last. I could see his eyes were pink and sore with drink and stress. He had grown a beard. It was wiry and wet with beer.

I put my arms up and held onto Ben's, trying to pull myself away from the bar. I couldn't bear for Tom to see me. I had no idea what he would do, what he might shout at me. I felt sick at the thought of all the things he could say, that someone with no restraint could throw at me.

'Wait a sec,' Ben said quietly. He held my arms firmly but without discomfort. 'Let's go round the back. Won't be hardly anyone in the snug.'

I was swallowing, starting to panic. 'What if he comes round there?' I croaked.

'He's just about to get chucked out. He won't be coming into the other bar,' he said calmly. I looked up at him. He had a kind confident look in his eye that I hadn't seen in a long time. 'You were doing so well Lucy. Come on. Let's not let him spoil a nice night out, eh?' I nodded silently and let him push me in front of him.

The snug was quieter. It only had a handful of the older villagers trying to escape the enthusiasm and noise of the main bar. We sat in an alcove at the back. I sat facing the door, checking that Tom did not come in.

'I don't think you need to worry about him, you know,' Ben said, picking up his bitter and taking a foamy sip.

I stared at him wordlessly, incredulous that he thought Tom Riley harmless.

'I know he was out of order coming round like that,' he said putting his hand up to acknowledge my concern, 'but I think he's an OK bloke.'

My temptation was to vehemently disagree with him. He hadn't seen his rabid face at the window, hadn't been alone while he prowled outside the house. I faltered though. Did I trust my memory and state of mind at the time, enough to disagree with Ben in all confidence?

Ben took my silence as agreement and carried on. 'He's one of the part-timers at the fire service you know. I get to see him on scenes quite a bit. He's a decent bloke.

Good at his job and well liked and all,' Ben said putting his case.

'Not on duty tonight then,' I said sarcastically.

Ben looked embarrassed. 'No,' he said looking down into his glass. 'He was handing over the keys to the garage today, tidying the last bits and pieces out.'

'Shit,' I said. I regretted my sarcasm and blushed. I hadn't heard that his business had been hit so badly that it had folded. 'I didn't know,' I said looking away.

'Yeah,' replied Ben. 'This case hasn't helped him any.'

*

Ben looked up from his glass. 'Mum said she hadn't seen you about lately,' he said, more upbeat.

'No,' I said. I smiled happy to move onto another subject, and also pleased that I had managed to avoid her. 'How is she?' I asked out of politeness.

'She's all right. Been raising money for this bench for Jake and that. She not managed to get you for that yet?' he said laughing.

'No. I'll put some money through the door,' I said frowning.

'So you don't think it's a good idea, this memorial fund then?'

I shook my head, trying to straighten my thoughts, rather than plainly disagreeing. 'I don't know. It doesn't matter what I think does it. If it makes her happy....' I shrugged.

'Yeah, I suppose. So been up to anything?' he asked tentatively, aware of what my old lifestyle had been.

'Yeah,' I said surprised at it myself. 'I've seen a lot of my neighbour.'

'Who? Karen?'

'Yes, and her son mainly, during the day.'

He raised his eyebrows, 'well stranger things have happened I suppose.' He nodded his head pushing out a sceptical lower lip.

I didn't have time to ask him what he meant before he carried on. 'Hey,' he said looking at me, his eyes wide and intense, 'You want to watch yourself there you know.'

'Why?' I said, confused.

He leant in closer, putting his head lower, conspiratorially. 'She's a lesbian you know.'

'What! That's bollocks,' I said immediately. I snapped my head up away from his gossip.

'No really,' he said, his eyes wide to emphasise his conviction.

'Really, that is such a load of bollocks,' I said laughing.

'Seriously.'

'She's got a husband, two kids, ….' I didn't think I needed to go on.

He crossed his arms, and smiled, pleased at himself. 'Well,' he carried on speaking in a low voice, 'a mate at the station plays football on the same team as him. And one time, one of the other blokes started ribbing him about him being a single bloke again, chasing the ladies. And then the bloke adds 'Just like his wife', he says.

'Apparently, he went mental. Had to be dragged off the other bloke. Poor bugger didn't know that Karen had been seeing a lady friend of hers like. Trod right in it there he did. He thought he was only joking. Nearly got the crap beaten out of him for it.' Ben nodded the authenticity of his knowledge. 'Bit of a nasty bastard, her husband by the sound of it,' he added frowning.

I stared at him, my mouth open, my palms turned up to indicate how ridiculous I thought it.

'I'm not lying,' he said, taking another drink.

I still couldn't believe it. I hadn't seen any evidence of it. I tried to think back to when she had related her affair to me. I was sure it had been with a man, a male friend of hers. Hadn't it?

'See,' he said raising his glass to my confused look.

'No, no, not at all,' I said frowning, trying to recall anything she had said that pointed to an affair with a woman.

'She'll have you I'm sure,' he said joking, grinning at me.

'Shut up,' I said, hitting him on the shoulder lightly. 'You really can't spread rumours like that in a place like Pennance.'

'I'm not. I'm just warning you. And that's only because she's obviously taken a shine to you,' he said still jesting.

I felt hurt when he said that. Karen's company had been the best thing in my life for a long time. I didn't like that it might be a source for gossip and speculation for him. I didn't like that he talked about her as a source of titillation. I started to get angry with him the more I thought about it, feeling protective of her.

'Why does it matter anyway?' I said, affecting a nonchalant attitude, trying to dampen my anger.

'Why's it matter?' It was his turn to look incredulous.

'Why does it matter if she sees women?' I shrugged.

'Cos….' he stuttered. 'Well because, you don't want some lezzer coming after you do you,' he said, looking offended that I hadn't realised this obvious point.

I laughed. I didn't laugh at what he said, or even at him. I laughed at the response that had come into my head. I'd thought that I didn't have to worry about Karen coming after me, because she was way out of my league. I didn't tell him though. I didn't think that he would find it amusing.

'Well, I'll keep my eye on her then,' I said sarcastically, laughing and not believing a word of his story.

He looked hurt at my disbelief and went to fill up our drinks, not looking pleased.

*

'You know, you should move up to the village,' he said putting the drinks down in front of me.

'Move?' I asked, confused. I couldn't think of anything more inconvenient.

'Yeah. There's a house for sale up near mine. Modern house. Not so pretty as the cottage mind. I know you like that kind of thing, but it looks a nice house.'

'I really don't want the hassle of moving at the moment,' I said feeling exhausted at the thought.

'Just, you know, you are quite isolated down there. And if you are worried about Tom, then surely you'd be better off up here, with people you know around you,' he said seriously.

I didn't understand where this had come from. One minute he was trying to reassure me that Tom was nothing to worry about, and the next he was stoking up my paranoia again. And, the thought of moving into the village to be surrounded by all the people Jake had known and to be closer to Margaret made me react physically against the idea.

'I'm OK where I am. And I've been feeling a lot better about it since Karen moved in,' I said to reassure him.

He was quiet for a moment. 'What's Karen going to do against the likes of someone like Tom Riley?' he said.

I looked at him in disbelief.

'Not that I think there's any harm in him. But if you're worried,' he said raising his eyebrows, indicating that I should think about it. 'Besides, weather's going to turn colder soon. Always starts to bite after Christmas. Nice central heating in new houses.'

'I'll manage,' I said, unimpressed with his reasons. I already had a pile of blankets down in the living room, ready to wrap around me on the colder days, and I think I had enough extreme outdoor clothing to manage in a Cornwall winter.

'And that cottage is going to be like an ice-box soon if you won't light that fire,' he added.

'Ben,' I said more firmly than I had meant to. I took a deep breath to calm myself. 'Thanks for letting me know. But I'm all right at the cottage.' I took a drink and looked away, not wanting to discuss it any further.

I didn't stay much longer, only long enough to chat about less emotive subjects so we could part on better terms. He accompanied me outside and I'm glad he did. Tom was passed out on the bench by the pub.

'Will you check he doesn't move while I leave? Check he doesn't register that it's me and follow me home,' I said quietly. I felt guilty requesting his help after being firm with him earlier.

'Course,' he said smiling. 'I'll give one of the guys on duty a ring, after you've gone, to come and sort him out, take him home.'

I unchained my bike from a lamp post and said good night to Ben. I hugged him goodbye clumsily, holding my bike with one hand and half hugging him with the other.

'You want to come out again sometime?' he suggested tentatively.

'Yeah,' I said sighing. 'That'd be nice.' I smiled a tired, closed lip smile at him.

2.

'I missed you,' Karen said, beaming at me when she opened the front door. She threw her arms around my shoulders and squeezed me tight, holding me for a few seconds so that I could feel her body beginning to warm mine. She released me from her embrace, although she still held me within arms length.

'You look really good today,' she said looking over my face. 'It suits you with your hair down like that. Although I like it tied up as well,' she said smiling.

I blushed at the compliment, but smiled at her, unreservedly glad to see her too.

'You've been very much missed these last few days, and not just by me,' she said.

I heard the rapid thud of feet from behind her and we both turned to see George emerge explosively from the sitting room.

'Look George, Lucy's here.'

I couldn't help but smile and laugh when he giggled and started jumping on the spot, stamping the floor in excitement.

'I don't think he'd say no to some football in the garden,' she said quietly. 'Do you fancy entertaining him while I put lunch out?'

She hadn't said it quietly enough. George had run into the sitting room, retrieved the silver football and was already running towards the back door.

'Wellies George!' she shouted after him, looking elated.

We sat round the table after lunch, drinking tea. It was a beautiful day, crisp and sparkling outside with sunlight flooding the kitchen. Karen sat leaning her elbows on the table with a cup in her hand. She had closed her eyes and was basking in the sunlight.

I'd tried to resist it, but I hadn't been able to stop myself thinking about what Ben had said. I found it difficult not to look at Karen in a different way, having to consider her as a sexual being after Ben's allegations about her sexuality.

I didn't find it unpleasant thinking of her in this light. It wasn't like the adjustment I'd had to make when Peter from work found a girlfriend. I'd found the idea of someone wanting to have sex with him, imagining someone wanting to undress and touch him, nauseating. It had taken a while for me adjust my image of him again, revert him back to his old asexual persona.

She had a beautiful face I thought, looking at her pale, sculptured cheeks in the sunlight. With her eyes closed, she reminded me of an alabaster bust, one where the surface was so smooth that you could hardly resist touching it. Her plump lips were spread in a content smile, enjoying the sunshine. Way, way out my league I thought to myself, amused again at Ben's concerns.

My eyes ran down her elegant neck and took in the hollow above her collar bone, imagining what it would be like to run my finger along her curves and down her slim chest. She wore a low-cut T-shirt, the top of her breasts rising out of it. I imagined my finger tips running down her chest, over the softness of the top of her breast and down beneath the cup of her bra. I tried to imagine what her nipples would look like and pictured my hand gently caressing her breast out of her bra to see her naked chest.

I blushed and coughed, embarrassed at my reassessment of her, surveying her in too intimate detail.

She opened her eyes, sat back in her chair and looked at me. Her eyes were clearer today, more focused. I could see who she was properly, instead of catching glimpses of her when she looked past me.

'Isn't it a lovely day,' she said sleepily. She stretched up her arms, reaching as high as she could with her fingers. Her T-shirt came un-tucked with the movement, revealing her soft belly, a vertical line down its centre inviting my mental touch further.

She felt soft, warm, as my finger tip explored her stomach, ran around the pale thin stretch marks, lower and lower until I ran my touch along the top of her jeans. She arched her chest and stomach forward enjoying her stretch more, a gap appearing at the top of her jeans. I could see the top of her white knickers, could imagine, slipping my finger under the elastic to find soft dark hair.

'Oh, that's better,' she said with pleasure, pushing her arms straight.

I gulped and twitched my eyes to look away from her and towards the window. I wondered if she had noticed my embarrassment or seen me peeking into her underwear. 'So how was your friend?' I stuttered, trying to distract her from noticing my blushes.

She dropped her arms and caved her body in, curling her shoulders over. The warmth disappeared from her face immediately. She frowned at the table in front of her. I was unnerved by her rapid change of mood and sorry that I had spoken.

'Not so great,' she said sadly. She stared out of the window, blinking, perhaps holding back tears. She held her hands limp in her lap. Her face seemed to droop and fall with her mood.

She shuffled in her chair and looked up at me from beneath her eyebrows. 'It was the friend who I had the affair with,' she said.

'Oh,' I said surprised. I felt a twinge of embarrassment at having inadvertently raised an awkward subject. 'Sorry, I didn't realise. I didn't mean to pry,' I said hastily.

'You're not,' she said. She reached over and squeezed my hand, holding it in hers while she thought for a moment or two. 'They wanted to start things again, where we had left off,' she said at last, slowly removing her hand.

I sat with my question filling my throat, holding it back from reaching the air. Had Karen started seeing this person again? Was the person a woman? Why else would she not be specific about seeing him, a man, a boyfriend?

'I didn't want to, and things got unpleasant,' she said frowning. She looked upset.

I felt a surprising number of feelings. Relief was one of them. I didn't want to lose Karen's good company, which inevitably I would if she started a relationship. I also recognised a small element of jealousy as well, which confused me. I didn't know if I was jealous or affronted by the lover demanding they start again.

I frowned, trying to put my emotions aside. 'I suppose it might be difficult with Sophia and George, but they will have to get used to you seeing people who aren't their dad,' I said neutrally.

'Oh it's not that,' she said looking up at me, 'although Sophia hated, Sophia hated my ex. And Sophia does know that I might see people other than David – he's made it perfectly clear that she will have to accept his girlfriends after all,' she said getting upset at remembering her husband. A tear ran down her cheek and she swiped it away quickly, embarrassed at her show of emotion.

'You don't have to explain anything,' I said quietly.

'No I want to. I, I....' She stopped dropping her head, laughing at herself. 'You must think me crazy. I'm all over the place today.' She wiped another tear that slid down her cheek.

I shook my head, trying to reassure her, wishing she wouldn't feel badly on my account.

'You see,' she hesitated, 'I've been trying to come off my medication, anti-depressants mainly. I started taking them to cope with the separation, but I want to feel myself again. Just, some days it all feels a bit much, that's all,' she said smiling apologetically.

I put out my hand to hold hers. She grabbed it tightly, squeezing it hard in her embarrassment. She breathed out long and noisily. 'I'm not much different most of the time, you know. I'm not going to turn into a raging lunatic or anything.'

I smiled at her, hoping that I hadn't been looking at her with an expression of fear or doubt.

'They just take the edges off,' she said, 'And sometimes everything is a bit sharp without them.' She squeezed my hand again and turned her face away as tears spilled over. She sniffed and breathed out a laugh. 'So, as long as you can ignore me blubbing every five minutes, I will be just the same as usual.'

I laughed with her and stood up beside her. She clutched my hand into her chest as I pulled her head into mine. I stroked down her hair, feeling the dark silky ribbons fall through my fingers. 'You can blub all you like,' I said gently and leant down to kiss the top of her head.

'Thank you,' she said as I sat down. She still held my hand for comfort. 'It's not all bad things you know,' she said earnestly. 'There are good things as well. Good feelings too,' she said smiling at me.

We both turned then at the characteristic sound of George running down the hallway. He careered around the door, stepped on to the rung at the bottom of my chair, pulled up grabbing my arms and dropped onto his bum on my lap. I gave him a mock affronted look, which he ignored and he continued to show off his latest dinosaur.

I looked at Karen. She was half laughing, half crying, before her mouth turned down, crying overwhelmed by all her emotions. She mouthed the word 'sorry' at me and got up to find some tissues. She blew her nose nosily at the back of the kitchen while George obliviously flew the new dinosaur through the air.

'Do you have any leave spare?' she said when she had recovered. She sat down and ruffled George's hair. 'I was thinking of taking this one for a walk along the coast while the weather's so crisp and sunny. Do you fancy spending the day with us sometime soon?'

'I'd love to,' I said. I smiled at her and looked at George. I wondered if Ben would have worried if he'd seen us then; two broken women, laughing and crying.

3.

Simon, my brother, came to see me, pleasantly surprising me just before Christmas. He was quite devious about arranging the visit. He phoned me early on the Saturday morning.

'What you up to today then?' he asked pleasantly, talking to me in a sleepy weekend way.

'Oh not much,' I said, 'catching up on a bit of work, listening to the radio....'

'Just having a quiet weekend pottering around?'

'Yeah,' I said smiling relaxed, 'that kind of thing.'

'Good,' he said abruptly. 'I wanted to come and see you, so I'll be round in about 5 hours,' and he hung up the phone.

I stood there in disbelief looking at my phone, outraged that he had tricked me. 'You bugger,' I said out loud, smiling at his cheek.

He had visited the cottage once before, not long after Jake and I had moved in. I felt conscious of its changed state since that visit and ashamed of it. I looked around the kitchen. It hadn't been cleaned for months. The table was still unusable, piled high with post and rubbish. I still hadn't washed up the pans from the last real meal that I had cooked. The floor still squelched and stuck to my shoes when I walked across it.

'Shit,' I said quietly, covering my face with my hands, feeling the heat of my blushing cheeks, embarrassed at what he would find on his arrival.

I started to clean. I soaked the pans in boiling hot water, fearful of the mould colonies that had grown, collapsed and grown again in several generations. I scooped the rubbish from the table into a bin bag and threw the rest of the post, bills and year-old newspapers into another. I had to take a paint stripper to the floor. Wiping the tiles had simply turned the dirt into a shining mud; it was much simpler to scrape and peel it away.

The windows were green on the inside, the algae flourishing in the shaded winter light and coolness of the cottage. I coated a whole loo roll in bright green, wiping away the living condensation from the panes of glass.

I estimated that I had time to clean the sitting room and stairs perhaps. I had to think hard to remember where we had kept the vacuum. My mind went quite peacefully blank when I first thought of fetching it. I found it in the spare bedroom upstairs, next to a pile of boxes that had never been unpacked. It was quite satisfying vacuuming the stairs. The carpet was a different colour where I dragged over the hose. The sitting room was the same, clearing dark clean tracks over the brown carpet where I pushed the vacuum back and forward.

I only had time to wipe the worst away from the bathroom floors and surfaces, gathering an unpleasant mix of dust and hair as I wiped over the previously white suite. I threw a large amount of green cleaning fluid down the loo, and hoped that it might get on with the rest for me.

I stood in the living room, looking around. It looked more hygienic if not tidy. Weak rays of sun shone through the trees and through the kitchen. They lit up the clouds of vapour from my breath as I stood recovering from the activity. I had a full set of thermals on and three layers of fleece on my torso. I knew my brother would think this a far from normal way to live.

I turned and looked at the fire. It was empty and brushed clean. I had cleared it away several months ago, unable to stand the sight of the embers and charred remains in the grate. There were still a few logs in the basket with some kindling ready to light. I stared at it, feeling sick and dizzy at the prospect of lighting a fire.

Karen always kept the stove running calmly when I visited. She never let me see her fill it or set it alight. I had got used to its safe comforting heat. But the thought of lighting an open fire, having to hold a flaming match in my hand, inhaling the smoke that would snake from the newspaper and kindling, started to make me feel ill. The back of my throat closed up at the memory of choking fumes. My nose and forehead felt full of thick black smoke, stringent plastic fumes and sulphurous choking roasting remains. I could almost taste it, that unforgettable aroma of burning hair and bones.

I spun away from the fire, feeling faint. I leant down, resting my hands on my knees, breathing heavily. I started to stumble towards the kitchen holding myself upright against the wall, groping my way along until I could reach the table. I sat down, feeling dizzy from hyperventilating.

My reaction had taken me by surprise, an unwelcome reminder that I was not recovered, not a normal person yet. I had started to think of myself as more robust, more myself, after seeing Karen most days and going to the pub with Ben. But I hadn't even attempted a journey in a car and lighting a fire was beyond me. It appeared that my phobias were still intact.

I stood up annoyed with myself. So I couldn't light a fire. Well I would have to live with that failing. I brought through the oil radiator and closed the door to the living room. My brother would have to put up with normal living standards in the kitchen only.

I felt better, proud that I hadn't let myself spiral into despair. I made myself a cup of sugary tea and listened to the radio waiting for my brother to arrive.

*

'Oh Luce,' Simon smiled an emotional smile as I met him at the door. 'You look like you again,' he said pleased and sad at the same time.

I grinned at him and stretched up to hug him. It was good to see him, especially by himself without the full emotional load of our parents and his wife.

He squeezed me gently and spun me from side to side not letting go. 'You're looking really great,' he said into my ear.

He let me go and I remembered my earlier irritation. I punched him gently on the shoulder. 'You bugger,' I said, joking. 'I shouldn't be talking to you. Manipulating me like that. Last time I speak to you on the phone. It's back to one-line emails again for you,' I said grinning at him.

He shrugged unrepentant.

*

'So how's things?' he asked, still tentatively, handling me with care. We sat at the kitchen table, drinking coffee and eating a slice of apple cake that Karen had given me. 'Eating well at least,' he said enjoying the cake.

'Oh my neighbour baked that,' I said quickly, not wanting to take the credit.

'Really?' he said in disbelief. 'That's so, so, WI,' he said confused.

'No it's not,' I said laughing. 'She's become quite a good friend. I eat over there quite a lot.'

'Well dining at your neighbours is still pretty strange,' he said smiling.

'Just because you haven't got a clue who your neighbours are, doesn't mean it's weird that I know mine,' I replied.

'I thought your neighbour died? I suppose someone else moved in.'

'Yes, her daughter a few months ago. She's very nice. She's got a couple of kids and stays at home at the moment so I see quite a lot of her,' I stopped, wondering what to tell him about Karen. I could have told him more, could have gushed about her, but I felt embarrassed somehow. 'She's been very kind,' I said. 'Stopped me going completely nuts at least,' I admitted.

He frowned. 'I was worried about you,' he admitted quietly.

'I know,' I said, 'and I'm sorry. And I'm also grateful that you didn't tell me and make a fuss.'

He nodded, accepting my thanks but not looking comfortable that he'd had to behave that way.

'How's Lynn and the bubbin?' I asked, trying to steer him onto a more cheery subject.

'They're great,' he said, his face rising with a smile. 'He can almost walk at last,' he said overjoyed. 'I know that sounds really unimpressive. I mean, how many babies do you know who don't learn to walk? But it's such a relief and so exciting to watch,' he said his eyes glazed.

'Thanks for the photos,' I said smiling. He'd emailed twenty or more pictures of the toddler grinning to show off his first teeth. 'How's mum and dad?' I asked more cautiously.

He looked more reticent. 'They're good. Apart from worrying about you. Sorry, but that's just how they are,' he said reaching out for my hand.

'No, it's OK, I asked.' I shrugged.

'They're coming down for Christmas. There is room if you want to come and stay too,' he said.

I had a knot in my stomach, thinking about my parents and their anxieties caused by me. I had feared them, worrying that I would break down and tell them everything. I don't know why, but telling them of my shameful flaws and actions would be the most crippling admission. I suppose if they had looked at me, repelled by my actions, I would have felt the ultimate rejection - disgusting the last people in the world who could still care for me. I felt the stress and tension freeze my chest imagining my confession.

I looked at him, pained by the thought of shutting them out more. 'Soon,' I said. 'I'm getting there,' I tried to reassure him.

'I got you a present,' he said standing up. He went out to the car and brought out an unwrapped games console. He was grinning as he handed it over. 'Lynn didn't think I should get you one, so I had to buy it on the way. Sorry it's not wrapped.'

'Wow, thanks. It is very generous,' I said pleased.

'No it's not that. She thought I shouldn't be encouraging you to stay in playing games. That you should be getting out socialising,' he said frowning. 'Do you like it? I know it's not a hard-core gaming type console but I just got one at home and it's great fun,' he said looking excited.

'No this is brilliant,' I said enthusiastically. 'I can play this with George,' I said turning over the box to look at the contents.

'George?' he tried to say innocently.

I didn't grasp his suspicion straight away. 'Oh, it's Karen's three-year-old,' I said frowning at him.

'Oh,' he replied, feigning disappointment. 'Not a local farm boy you've taken on as your secret lover?'

'No,' I said irritated with him but smiling.

He blushed, perhaps feeling awkward that he had suggested that I could have moved on since Jake.

He stayed a couple of hours before getting ready to go back. He took a photo of us on his phone, holding the phone at arms length and squeezing my cheek into his so that we would fit in the frame. It was funny looking at it. We didn't look that different from the photos of us when we were younger, grinning stupidly at the camera.

'Mum and dad will love it,' he said pressing a button to save it.

I saw him out to the car. I was kissing him good bye when Karen drove past. I waved at her and she smiled briefly, but she didn't stop. I'd wanted to introduce her to Simon, to reassure him further. I wanted to impress him that I was keeping such good company. I saw Sophia looking out of the back window as they drove past. She smiled and waved which I didn't expect.

4.

Karen looked tired when she answered the door. She frowned and looked tense, crossing her arms in front of her.

'I'm sorry, Sophia's at home today,' she said, not quite looking me in the eye. 'I thought it was the last day of term today, but it's a training day for staff, and the kids are home for Christmas now.'

I looked at her blankly and then shrugged. 'That's OK. No problem,' I said. 'We can go for a walk another day. I'll let you get on with spending a bit of time with Sophia,' I said, turning to leave.

She looked at me unflinchingly in the eyes. I thought she tried to look for something. I don't know if she found it, but she looked away and at her feet. 'I told George that you'd be coming though,' she said. 'He'll be disappointed.'

I didn't know what to say. I didn't know if she was trying to persuade me to leave or to spend the day with them. I hesitated, waiting for her to direct me.

'I suppose Sophia can't object to a friend spending the day with us though can she,' she said as a statement.

I thought I understood then. I assumed Sophia had been difficult that morning, not wanting to share her mother on her day off. 'It's up to you,' I shrugged, 'You know best,' I said smiling to let her know I was fine with whatever she chose.

She looked at me again, still not seeming to find what she looked for in my face. She pursed her lips together trying to smile. 'Let's go for a walk then.'

I'd expected Sophia to be in an especially petulant mood from Karen's behaviour, but she seemed no worse than usual. I walked ahead with her up the slope through the wood to the coastal path, while Karen trailed behind accompanying George's small steps.

'We're not going to get very far with George are we?' she tutted looking back down through the trees.

I laughed at her impatience with her sibling. I remembered Simon being unimpressed by my physical limitations when I was little, too small to catch a ball properly or to run and play football. 'He'll be quicker when he makes it through the trees, it's much flatter for a bit now,' I said, looking ahead over the familiar coastline. She was right though. It was going to be slow going.

She looked at me, unconvinced of what I said.

I smiled and then looked away, pretending to admire the view across the dark rippled sea. The weather had started to turn. It was still icy, but it was starting to get windy now and it was grey overhead.

'I don't know why we're going on this stupid walk anyway. I'm cold,' she said tucking her hands under her armpits.

I shivered involuntarily. I hadn't worn enough clothes for standing around waiting on the exposed cliffs. I'd stupidly assumed we'd be walking my usual brisk pace. 'It is bloody cold,' I agreed with her.

She smiled and seemed to relax, perhaps because I had agreed with her or because I swore.

'Where do you come from? You're not from around here are you?' she said.

I didn't understand her line of questioning but was happy to answer her. 'No, I grew up in London,' I said.

'Why did you leave?' she asked. 'Why did you come here?'

'I went to university in Exeter, and I suppose I liked the South West, so I stayed,' I shrugged.

'Was that your boyfriend we saw you with?' she asked equally directly, smiling as if the question gave her pleasure in some way.

I was taken aback by her continuous questioning and also confused about who she referred to. I said 'no' automatically and then 'I don't know who you mean.'

'The man we saw you kissing outside your cottage,' she said.

I laughed. 'No, that's my brother. Couldn't you see the resemblance?' I said surprised. 'Maybe not, we both look like average white English types I suppose.'

'But you do have a boyfriend,' she persisted, looking more like her usual self, verging on showing teenage distaste for my answers.

I breathed in deeply and then admitted 'No, I don't have a boyfriend at the moment,' I said uncomfortably.

'Sophia, don't be so rude. They're very personal questions to ask.' Karen had appeared at the top of hill and lifted a very padded George over the stile. He only had an inch of his face exposed to the cold air. His arms were rounded off with large mittens and his head was hidden by a fleece hat with flaps down his cheeks which were tied under his chin.

I smiled at the sight of George. 'It's OK,' I said shaking my head, not wanting to cause any awkwardness between Karen and Sophia. We turned around and started walking slowly along the path, Karen holding George's hand while Sophia and I ambled along in front.

'So how long is it since you had a boyfriend?' she asked after a few steps.

I was starting to be shaken by her persistence, but I tried to satisfy her curiosity. 'Over a year ago,' I said succinctly.

'Why did you split up?' she said looking expectantly at me. I thought I saw her almost smile. She had a look in her eye, as if she knew that the answer was a cause of discomfort to me. I felt manipulated.

I blinked and looked away from her. 'He died in a car crash.' I said, swallowing.

'Sophia!' Karen shouted from behind us. I stopped, waiting for Karen to catch up but Sophia kept walking. Karen looked furious, frowning after her. 'I'm really sorry,' she said, the force of anger still in her voice.

'I didn't realise that was your brother,' Karen said almost sheepishly. We were strolling slowly with George stumbling in front of us. Sophia had marched ahead, a hundred metres or so, by herself. 'I would have stopped to say hello if I'd known,' Karen continued looking apologetic

'It was a last-minute decision of his,' I said excusing her. 'I didn't know that he was visiting until he was in the car just about to set off,' I laughed remembering his cheek. 'I would have loved you to meet him otherwise.'

'Are you going to visit your family over Christmas?' she asked.

I looked guilty. 'No. I, I find it difficult being with them all still. Too much undeserved sympathy,' I said.

She nodded understanding my predicament and squeezing my arm in comfort. 'Would you like to come over on Christmas Day? It'll just be me. I've agreed with David that he can have the kids at Christmas and I'll have them back for New Year.'

'I'd love to,' I said enthusiastically. She looked sad at the prospect of not seeing George and Sophia and I wanted her to be happy.

'I was just thinking I'd get a chicken in, a simple roast,' she said. 'Perhaps have some wine now I'm off the drugs. Watch some crappy films. Do you fancy that?' she asked, looking at me hopefully.

'I can't think of a better way to spend the day,' I smiled.

'This is ridiculous!' shouted Sophia, marching back towards us, interrupting our arrangements. 'We're on the flat and we're still going along like snails. I'm cold!' she whined.

'All right,' I said loudly and cheerily. 'Come here George.' I leant down, picking him up under his arms and lifted him onto my shoulders, just about able to take his weight if I picked him up in one smooth movement.

I heard a giggle from above me, and assumed George was happy with the arrangement. Karen laughed and looked up at him, holding his small hand to check he was stable. 'We all ready to go?' I asked Karen, keeping my arms up holding George's hands. She beamed at me and nodded.

Sophia looked horrified. She tutted at the scene and turned on her heel. I blushed at her disapproval of my over-familiarity with George.

We walked for about half a mile, George enjoying the view from my shoulders and Karen pacifying Sophia by accompanying her a few steps ahead. I had to put him down again when we reached a sharp incline down to a sandy cove. I didn't want to risk slipping and dropping him from such a height.

Instead, Karen took George by one hand and I took the other, and we swung him down the slope in huge jumps and steps. He squealed and laughed with delight at being lifted up into the air, his legs swinging beneath him. Karen picked him up and carried him on her hip up the short slope on the other side. She looked exhausted and red-faced by the top of the spur.

'Take your brother a sec Sophia,' she said putting him on the ground. Sophia reluctantly took her brother's small hand and led him in small slow steps to the highest point of the spur.

Karen stood up and stretched her back forwards, breathing heavily. 'He's getting a bit big for that,' she said, the sound of her breath pitching higher as she stretched her mouth to smile.

I turned around to see how far we'd come. I could see the buildings of Pennance clearly still and almost make out my white-washed cottage in the trees in the valley that led down to the sea.

'We still haven't got very far have we,' Karen said laughing.

'Doesn't matter does it?' I said.

'I was hoping we would go a reasonable distance. We must have only covered where you usually go running,' she said.

'I don't mind. I never get bored of this coastline. It looks different every day,' I said, watching the greys of the sea darken and swirl with the changing cloud overhead. Streaks of shimmering silver lit the grey water where the sun broke through the cloud in thin cuts. We watched a beam of sunlight narrow and fade as another one blinked open on another patch of sparkling water.

*

'Where's George?' Karen shouted towards Sophia. I turned around concerned at the tone of her voice. Sophia's back was turned towards us. She was looking out from the top of hill over the cliffs, her hands stiff by her sides, empty.

Karen ran the few steps between them, stopping abruptly at the cliff top. I was just a second or two behind her. I automatically looked down the cliff. It was covered with gorse bushes as far as I could see, with very little exposed rock but it was still extremely steep. It was only fifteen metres high, but I couldn't see the foot of the cliff. It must have been increasingly sheer towards the bottom.

I looked at Sophia. She looked shocked, her mouth open, her eyes fixed looking down the cliff.

'Where's George?' Karen shouted, her voice tightening higher with panic.

Sophia looked up at her mother, her eyes wide with fear.

I stepped closer to the cliff edge, dreading Sophia's response. About half way down, I could see a small fleecy hat, caught on a gorse bush, the ear flaps still tied together.

5.

'Wait,' I said grabbing Karen's arm. She was about to start lowering herself down the cliff, panicking, instinctively wanting to rescue her child. I doubted she was thinking clearly. The slope was steep and there was no way to secure her if she climbed down. She would have to descend too far for us to hold her. I looked around trying to see if there were any paths or vantage points for a better view of where he might have fallen before taking that dangerous route.

'Go to the cove,' I said pointing down to the sandy beach we had passed. 'See if you can see him from there. I'll go and see if I can spot anything from the next bay.'

Karen ran towards the beach, Sophia walking a few steps behind her. I'd hoped that the coastline would bend in a favourable way so that I might be able to see the bottom of the cliff, but my view was blocked by a buttress of grey rock. I ran back to the top of the spur and looked down the vegetated cliff.

I could see Karen and Sophia on the beach, desperately trying to peer around the cliffs from their vantage point. Their demeanour told me that they could not see him.

I stretched my leg down from the path in between the gorse bushes. The earth was steep beneath it, falling away at such a steep angle that I had to kick my heels in to make a tiny ledge for my foot. I grabbed on to the twisted branch of gorse, my arms quickly becoming lacerated with tiny scratches from the bush's spikes. I scraped my other leg down, pushing my heels into the steep gravelly soil, trying to find a grip.

I descended cautiously for several metres, grabbing from one bush to the next lowering myself down. I couldn't see my feet beneath the plant cover. I had to trust that they were secure on solid ground beneath.

The cliff started to bulge out becoming more convex and the incline becoming steeper still. I peered out, stretching away from the gorse bush I held, trying to see any sign of George. I could see the grey water below, swelling and curdling beneath me, but I still couldn't see the foot of the cliff where the land and sea met. I saw nothing of George.

I stepped down again, pushing an exploratory leg down, trying to find my next foothold. I must have been at the lip of where the cliff had been eaten away by the sea, at the top of a small cave. I'd thought that I had found a small ledge of solid stone sticking out of the soil, and started to put my full weight on it, when the stone crumbled away from my feet, falling vertically into the water below. I didn't have the strength to take my weight on the branch that I held. My hand ripped painfully along the bark and over the spiny foliage.

I felt my stomach swirl as I tumbled through the air, my body feeling weightless for a moment. I didn't have time to feel fright or worry at where I might land, just enough time to realise that I was falling.

I plunged into the grey sea, icy water flooding around every part of my body in an instant, freezing between my legs, my stomach, over my head, into my ears, down my neck and back. I swallowed water as I took a sharp breath in with shock. It felt like my heart stopped, my chest clenching with the sudden cold. I kept plunging down and down, and then I felt my buoyancy start to counteract my fall, feeling still and suspended in the water, my ears cold and deafened by the surrounding sea.

I kicked frantically, my legs feeling clumsy with my heavy boots on my feet, the clinging fabric of trousers hindering my movement. I desperately tried to control my panic to stop myself from coughing or breathing in more water. I felt the rising tension of my body fighting for breath, it telling me to open my lungs to air. I willed my way to the surface, feeling my ascent quicken and the weight of water suddenly lift as I rose to the surface.

I felt the icy wind on my face as I broke through, and coughed out harsh salty water. I swallowed a mouthful, feeling its chill in my throat as I bobbed up and down on the surface. My eyes were sore in the salty wind and I had to blink and strain to keep my eyes open. I was facing out to the grey sea and sky and had to twist and kick to turn around. I saw George floating by a rock under the overhang of the cliff. He floated up and down with the waves, his small hands clinging on to the top of a rock. His face was white with shock and cold.

'George!' I shouted, half in delight that I had found him conscious and looking largely unhurt. I swam towards him in a heavy mix of breaststroke and doggy paddle, my jacket sleeves dragging my movement. I grabbed the same rock as George with one hand and held him with the other, making sure he did not drift away in the heaving water.

I tried to decide if we should stay where we were, and wait for Karen to find help. We risked floating out to sea if we started swimming. I was a strong enough swimmer but I wasn't sure if I could safely reach the shore with George.

I looked at him weakly clinging to the rock. His hair was dark and soaked onto his head, trailing in dark wet ribbons around his face. His small pink mouth was open and trembling. He had been in the water several minutes by then.

'George, we're going, to have to swim, to the beach,' I said, straining my head up and out of the water, coughing out the water that broke on the cliffs beside us, showering us.

'Do you understand?' I shouted.

He looked at me, his eyes clear and fixed on mine. He nodded.

'You're going to lie on your back in the water and kick, yeah? I'll pull you along and keep you floating, but you must keep kicking.' I wanted him to keep moving, to generate some heat more than helping us swim.

I unzipped my jacket beneath the water and pulled it off, discarding it to float away in the water. I let go of the rock and took George's hands, pulling him along on his belly.

'Start kicking George,' I shouted.

He tired quickly and looked exhausted by the time we cleared the cave under the cliff. I pulled him towards me, and then put my hand under his chin to keep him afloat.

'Backwards, George,' I said struggling to speak, the water filling my mouth as we rose and fell in the waves. I turned onto my side, paddling in the water with my free hand, kicking under the waves, dragging him along on the surface.

We made slow progress. I wished I'd discarded more clothes; the drag of the water on them was draining me. The sides of the cliff moved slowly, the waves taking us forwards and then dragging us back so that our progress was taken away from us. I could see Karen on the beach though, a wave pushing her into view before blinking her away again behind a rock.

I wanted to say something encouraging to George, to keep kicking, we were nearly there. But I had no spare breath or energy. My lungs were raw with the cold salty air and the exertion.

I think we must have battled another five minutes before I felt the sandy floor with my kicking feet. I'd never felt so relieved to feel the spongy ground take my weight. I stood up in the water, exhausted, holding George from the waves. I couldn't lift him properly. I half dragged him through the surface.

Karen ran into the water and grabbed him from me. I tripped and fell on my knees as I watched her carry him on to the beach. I was much colder out of the water. The wind was sharp and was chilling me to my core. 'Get him dry,' I shouted, realising George's small form would chill more quickly than mine.

Karen was stripping him as I walked up the beach out of the water. She ripped off her fleece jacket wrapping it around him, trying to dry his shivering body. His lips were blue now and he seemed unaware of what was happening.

'Give him your jacket and hat,' I said in between breaths to Sophia. She stood watching the scene, her face still paralysed with shock. She looked up at me blankly. 'Give him your jacket Sophia,' I said as clearly as I could. I found speaking difficult. My cheeks and lips were numb and I couldn't control them to form the right shapes. She looked at me, up and down with disgust. I looked down and saw that I was dribbling water and saliva, my mouth too numb to notice it. 'Now!' I shouted at her, making a strained noise, although audibly furious at her attitude.

She reluctantly took off her coat and hat handing it Karen to wrap around George, discarding the now wet fleece on the floor.

'You should run ahead and put pans of water and the kettle on,' I said to Sophia more gently. 'Get a warm water bottle ready for your brother,'

She looked at me stubbornly, unwilling to take orders from me. I stared at her, incredulous at her lack of cooperation.

'Go on Sophia!' I heard Karen say desperately, handing her the key. 'For God sake's run,' she shouted at Sophia's inertia.

*

The walk back was excruciatingly slow. Karen had to keep resting, tiring quickly carrying George's limp weight. I struggled to keep up with them though. My legs were cold right through and didn't work properly. My muscles felt like they tore against each other, seizing up. I thudded along the path, my feet numb and clumsy, jarring my cold body as I misjudged contact with the ground.

Karen was crying when she reached the manor, frustrated at her slow journey home and George's delirious state. She went straight through to the living room, I assume to warm him by the stove.

'Get Lucy some towels and my dressing gown,' I heard her shout.

I stood in the hallway, exhausted, my movements and thoughts beginning to retard. I felt tired, so incredibly tired. My eyelids would take a second too long to open when I blinked. It felt like I was falling asleep on my feet. I had stopped shivering and I felt too tired to jump up and down to warm myself.

Sophia stood in front of me with a pile of white towels. I took them from her, but my hands were numb and I dropped them on the floor. I mumbled something about telling her not to worry and I knelt down to untie my shoelaces, intending to undress.

I couldn't control my fingers. I thought clearly that I wanted to pinch my fingers together to hold my laces, but my hands wouldn't respond. I tried willing them to squeeze, but they seemed detached from me. They were so numb that I wasn't sure that the hands I looked at were my own. I tried to hold the lace squeezed between the palms of my hands but the lace slipped through and became ensnared in a wet knot.

I stood up, having to reach out to the wall to steady myself. 'I can't undo my clothes,' I slurred to Sophia. I meant to ask her to fetch her mother, but I couldn't form the words. She stood in front of me, staring at me with a neutral expression, that looked like it could flicker into scorn, laughter or hate in an instant.

My mind blinked, going black for a second. I wobbled on my feet. 'Please,' I said pleading with her to fetch her mother. She looked at me as if I was something unpleasant and stepped forward. She knelt down and undid my shoe laces, then reached up to undo the button of my trousers having to tug at the waistband to loosen the soaked fabric from around the catch. She unzipped my trousers and then stood up to undo the buttons of my shirt. She stepped back, repelled by her intimate aide, but continued to stare at me.

I peeled off my clothes, letting them fall and slap the floor. I wavered, leaning down to pick up the towels and slowly started to rub my numb body dry. I moved so slowly. Just lifting my head seemed to take five times longer than it should.

'Put this on,' Sophia said curtly.

She held out a dressing gown, open and ready for me to slide my arms in. I stumbled forward, slotting my arm in, my numb hands snagging on the sleeves. I turned my back to her rolling into the gown and then found the other arm with some difficulty. I held the front together under my arms. I didn't attempt to tie the belt in a knot.

'Are those from the accident?' she said behind me.

I took a long time to respond. I couldn't think what she referred to.

'Those scars on your back,' she said, running her hand down the back of the dressing gown.

I nodded slowly, my head swirling with the movement. I became confused then, uncertain of what I did and what people said.

*

Karen must have come to fetch me and taken me into the sitting room. I can't imagine I would have got there any other way. I was only vaguely aware of my surroundings when the doctor arrived. George was making noises again, starting to form words.

I felt overwhelmingly tired, drifting in and out of sleep, being constantly woken by Karen or the doctor. They kept telling me to drink some warm water even though I wasn't thirsty.

The doctor kept taking thermometer readings, not letting me rest until my temperature slowly rose to within a degree or two of normality.

I was covered in blankets and I remember Karen dried my hair with a hair drier.

I heard snippets of conversation. The doctor told Karen to watch me and George and call him if she saw any change at all. I think I heard the front door shut when he left.

I heard Karen and Sophia's voices at one point, sounding more distant. Perhaps they were in the hallway.

'What the hell happened, Sophia? You were meant to be watching him.'

'It wasn't my fault. He let go of my hand.'

'Sophia, he could have died. Your brother could have died! You should have been holding him.'

'It's not my job to look after him. You should have been looking after him, not talking to her.'

*

It was dark when I woke, the first time when my thoughts felt clear and I didn't drift back to sleep instantly. The stove was glowing gently in front of me. I must have been on the sofa for several hours by then, but I felt warm at last.

I felt snug in Karen's dressing gown. Its soft material had risen up around my face and it smelled of her. It was comforting and it made me smile. I could feel my hands and feet again. I squeezed my fingers beneath the blanket, relieved that they were back under my control. All my senses seemed to be returning. I ached though, throughout my whole body. It was painful when I sat up.

Karen was sitting on the armchair, George asleep in a blanket on her lap. She smiled at me, seeing me awake. She got up slowly, turning round to put George back on the chair. He didn't blink or even make a noise at the disturbance.

'How you feeling?' she said quietly, kneeling down in front of me.

I laughed quietly. I felt awful. My body felt heavy and as if someone had been kicking me all over. 'How's George?' I asked, looking towards him concerned.

'He's good,' she said smiling. 'He recovered quicker than you. I think we got him wrapped up just in time to stop the worst,' she said looking towards him.

She turned back. 'How amazing were you?' she said. She smiled but tears started to appear in her eyes. She reached up her hand and held my cheek. 'You were incredible,' she said.

I blushed at her gratitude and shook my head. 'I was just looking for him, and I slipped. I saved him by accident,' I said not wanting to take the unjustified credit.

'Will you listen to yourself,' she said amused and despairing. She put her other hand to my cheek, holding my face in her hands. 'You saved George's life. You can't tell me you didn't do that,' she said. She drew closer and kissed me, pressing her lips firmly into mine and then leaned back again. 'You were amazing.'

Part 5
1.

It was Christmas Eve a couple of days after the incident. I had to go into Pennance for a last meeting before Christmas with the solicitors together with Tom Riley, Margaret and Ben. I had been dreading facing Tom, even in the company of the lawyers and Jake's family. I think he recognised that I was the weak one, the one most likely to drop the case. I still feared his attention and persecution.

I set off from the cottage allowing the usual time that it took for me to cycle to Pennance. I hadn't taken account of my state after the hypothermia though. I hadn't recovered completely. In fact, I felt the after-effects for several days.

By the top of the lane I was already out of breath. I had to let the bike come to a stop and put my foot down to the ground to rest. It felt like I couldn't take enough air into my lungs. I expanded my chest out to its full extent taking in great volumes of air. It felt as if the air contained too little oxygen. My legs were weak and fatigued and I had broken into a cold sweat that made me feel vulnerable, remembering how debilitating the cold had been to me a couple of days before.

I had to push my bike up the hill to Pennance. It took me half an hour longer to get into the village than I'd accounted for.

We were meant to be meeting in the small community centre, just behind the supermarket, neutral ground between the Arundells and Rileys and their solicitors. I passed the community centre front doors on my way to the cycle rack and parking spaces. I had to pause when I came to a stop, recovering my breath to take the dizziness and fatigue away.

I was leaning down chaining up my bike, when I heard the double doors of the centre crash open. I looked up automatically to see the source of the noise. I froze when I saw Tom Riley. He stood outside the doors, letting them flap in and out noisily behind him. He looked furious. I could see his face was red beneath his greasy hair and beard. I stayed motionless, dreading that he might see me out of the corner of his eye if I moved.

He stood stiff, clenching his fists by his sides, curling his fingers in and out of his palms. He looked at the floor, casting his agitated eyes quickly from side to side. 'For fuck's sake!' he shouted and then took a swinging kick to the cigarette bin beside the doors. The metal bin clattered loudly across the road in front of the centre. He watched it tumble across the tarmac and then stared at it intently when it came to a rest, his chest heaving up and down with large angry breaths.

I watched him, paralysed, and saw his breathing slow and his chest subside into more even breaths. He continued to stare, his eyes wide, as he reached into his jacket for a cigarette. He blinked as he crunched his lighter into a flame and took a deep drag on his cigarette to start it smoking. He took another drag, blowing a large grey plume into the cold air and started to stare at nothing in front of him. He absently flicked the filter of the cigarette with his thumb to get rid of the ash.

His eyes came into focus and he lifted his head up straight. He took one last drag on the cigarette, threw it aside, and turned abruptly away in the opposite direction to me and started to walk quickly up the driveway to the main road.

My knees hurt when I stood up, having become seized from crouching beside the bike. I felt sick at witnessing Tom's outburst, realising how easily that could have been directed at me had he seen me. My hands were trembling as I pulled open the door to the community centre.

'Here she is!' Margaret shouted across the hallway.

She was standing around a table with our solicitor and another man who I assumed was Tom's. They shook hands and the man I didn't recognise picked up a square briefcase and strode towards me. He was frowning as he approached and gave me a cursory nod as he passed.

'Where's Ben?' I said confused as I approached Margaret.

'Oh, he's been and gone. He's probably home by now,' said Margaret jovially. 'I'm sorry we started without you. Couldn't get you on the mobile. Ben tried a dozen times, I could swear to it. We had no idea how long you were going to be, or whether you were going to make it at all. Need to get on with Christmas shopping in Plymouth see, and I need to get a move on.'

'But,' I tried to get a word in. 'So what have you agreed? Have we settled?' I asked confused.

'No. Tom's saying he's almost bankrupt and won't raise the offer any more. Says he can't afford it. Well, I asked him about all the money from the sale of the garage. That must have raised a tidy sum I said. Says it all went on clearing the backlog of wages and debts and repaying the mortgage. Not that I believe a word of it mind, the amount they used to charge. So we'll go to court,' she said lightly but determined.

I was shocked by her levity at squeezing the last money out of the man. I was tempted to believe that he was almost at his financial limit, given his extreme behaviour and the state of him in general.

'But, I was happy with the last offer,' I said, shocked that Ben and Margaret had decided to progress the case without me. 'In fact,' I said breathing in deeply, 'I think this has gone far enough. He's lost his business. What's there to gain from this?'

She looked surprised by my dissent, putting her head back and straightening her spine, squeezing double folds beneath her chin. Her eyes were glassy with annoyance and she stared at me, willing me to relent.

She spoke slowly and deliberately. 'He killed Jake.'

I blinked as she said it, a wave of guilt washing over me, my resolve dissolving with it. That flicker of doubt was enough. She won, as she always did. The case had too much momentum with Margaret's wilful witch hunt. There was little I could do to stop it other than lie outright in court.

She smiled her strained smile at me, the one where her eyes showed her real emotion. 'Well, that's that then,' she said, her shoulders and chest deflating as she relaxed into her victory.

'I won't sign anything,' I said meekly.

'Don't need you to,' she said matter of fact.

I turned slowly to leave when she caught my arm. I felt sick at her touch. 'I hear you've been quite the hero, saving Karen's boy.'

I felt almost violated that she knew, nauseous that nothing could happen within a mile of Pennance without her knowing. I tugged my arm away as gently as I could, trying not to reveal my repulsion.

'It was nothing,' I said petulantly, turning to leave, 'Anyone would have done the same.'

'Funny you two being friends though isn't it,' she said calling after me.

I could feel my stomach turn, fearing that she might repeat Ben's gossip about Karen's sexuality. It was none of her business who I spent my time with now Jake was gone or the nature of that friendship I thought stubbornly. I carried on walking out of the hall, pretending that I hadn't heard her.

Cycling back home was easier. I could free-wheel out of Pennance, and most of the way was downhill. I stewed, annoyed with Margaret for pressing the case through.

I was still distracted, annoyed about her prying questions about Karen, when I opened the cottage door. I was putting my bag down on the mat, when I became aware that something did not feel right about the cottage. I stood up alert, trying to detect what was different. I looked around the kitchen. Nothing seemed out of place. The table was clear, the kitchen tops had my plate and mug from breakfast, jars of coffee, tea, beans and old pasta were arranged as I'd expect on the shelves.

I listened intently, my ears feeling stiff as I strained to detect any sounds that did not belong to the cottage. I held my breath. My heart was beating strongly. I felt warm holding my breath, my face heating up from the exertion now I was out of the cold air. I couldn't hear anything though, just the whisper of the sea down the valley. I exhaled noisily, the back of my throat stretching out with my body's will to breathe.

I frowned. The cottage felt different to how I expected. I was still tempted to call out, to ask if anyone was there. I slowly and quietly stepped through to the sitting room. The sofa was empty, my desk chair unoccupied, the carpet was clear. No-one was there. I peered up the stairs, looking as far left and then right as I could, watching for any shadows changing on the landing at the top of the stairs.

I could feel my heart beating strongly still. My eyes were wide. I could feel my body was alert, ready to run at any provocation. I needed to check upstairs. I wouldn't be able to relax until I had checked the entire house. I looked at the stairs. They would creak as soon as I stepped on them. I would not be able to take an intruder by surprise if I walked cautiously up the steps.

I readied myself, not sure whether my body would simply turn and desert the cottage any second. I looked up the stairs and then leapt up the steps two at a time. I jerked my head left to look in the bedroom quickly scanning over the open wardrobe, the empty bed, under the small antique dressing table. Nothing was unexpected. I quickly turned right, opening the spare bedroom door violently, exposing myself wide-eyed to whatever might be in there. Grey cardboard boxes and the vacuum cleaner remained unmoved. I slammed the door shut again and stepped into the bathroom, throwing back the shower curtain, the last place anyone could be hidden. I found nothing and then I felt foolish rampaging around my own quiet home that appeared as normal.

I stood feeling stupid, the musty air beginning to fill my nostrils now that I stood still and breathed more calmly. That's when I realised what had been different. I hadn't been gone long, but long enough for my nose and mouth to become accustomed to clean outside air. The cottage always smelled damp when I came home, the air feeling moist and musty. It hadn't today. It hadn't been any different to outside. It had been aired, a door or window being left open, while I had been out.

I rattled the bathroom window. It was secure. I checked the spare room and bedroom; neither had been left open, or on the catch. I rushed back downstairs, checking the sitting room and kitchen windows.

Only the front door stood wide open. I tried to remember unlocking it when I got back. I had been too distracted to remember it clearly. I'd had other things on my mind. But surely if it had been unlocked, that would have shaken me and grabbed my attention as something out of the ordinary.

I stood staring at the door. No-one could have broken into the house and left all the windows tightly shut and the door locked. I was thinking quite clearly, rationally. I had no other explanation. I had to make myself accept that I was being oversensitive, perhaps from seeing Tom Riley again. I had to calm down and not be so paranoid.

I tried to laugh at myself, told myself out loud to stop overreacting. I smiled, and closed and locked the front door, not wanting to turn my back on it until it was secured. Starting to relax, I went through to the sitting room and took off my jacket. I hung it on a hook at the bottom of the stairs and then went over to the heater to switch it on to start drying the clothes on the rack beside it. That's when I froze again, this time certain that someone had been in the house.

There was a gap on the washing rack; a square space where a T-shirt should have been drying. I knew which one it should have been as well. It was my running T-shirt, a faded grey blue with a logo, a silhouette of a stylised mountain range. I knew for certain that I had washed it. I had washed all of my running clothes that day.

My whole body felt numb with fright, but my mind was not paralysed. It rapidly came to a logical conclusion that someone had been in the house, that they had taken my T-shirt, and that they must have had a key. It went blank when I tried to think who it could have been though.

My first instinct was to think of Tom Riley. But I couldn't think how he could get a key. Had I ever left my full set of keys with the garage? I usually took off the car key from the rest of the key-ring didn't I? I was almost sure that I did this. How else could he get a key?

Ben had a spare. Jake had given him one when we moved into the cottage, so we could easily get a copy if we locked ourselves out. Could he have taken it from Ben? I scrabbled around in my bag for my mobile. I had one missed call from Ben. I felt annoyed with Margaret for exaggerating their efforts at reaching me. I shook my head, trying to get rid of her image, a distraction. I pressed the buttons to return the missed call.

He answered after several rings.

'Hello?'

'Hi Ben. It's me,' I said.

'Been trying to reach you. You didn't turn up to the meeting,' he said.

'Yes I know,' I said irritably.

'Everything all right?' he asked.

'Yes, yes. Look, do you still have a spare key to the cottage?' I asked hurriedly.

'Probably yes,' he said as if he hadn't thought of it for a long time. 'You locked yourself out?' I could hear he was smiling at the prospect.

'No. I, I just wanted to know if you still had it. To check you hadn't lost it.'

'Oh I'm sure it's not lost,' he amiably.

'Can you check please,' I said.

'Yes course. You sure you're all right?' he said starting to sound concerned.

'Yes, yes, I'm fine. Could you just check quickly for me,' I said trying not to sound too frantic.

'Well I can check for you later. I'm not at home right now,' he said lazily.

'Oh. I thought Margaret said you were on your way home,' I said indignant.

He hesitated. 'Well, I'm not,' he said quite plainly.

*

I felt agitated and impatient waiting for Ben to phone back. I didn't want to press him, to try to hurry his search, in case he started to question me. I knew he would make me out to be paranoid, and would try to dissuade me that anyone had been there.

    I found myself staring at the computer on the desk by the window, a colourful ball bouncing around the screen. I stepped over to the desk, opening the lid of a white cardboard box at the back by the wall. I searched inside, through a pile of pencils, cabling, an old internet hub, a hard-drive. I found what I was looking for: a small webcam that I had never set up. I wiped my thumb across it, clearing away the dust.

    I fixed the camera on the frame of the door from the kitchen to the sitting room, hoping its wide-angle could capture any intruder coming in the front door and also anyone looking in through the kitchen windows.

    It didn't take me long to hook up the camera to the frame and trail the cable around the door frame to the floor, along the top of the skirting board and up behind my desk. I set the camera software to capture and save an image every second, hoping that would be frequent enough to catch a good image of the intruder. I set a program running to copy batches of the images to my computer at work as a backup and then clear them away every week to stop the photos filling up the computer.

    I sat back, feeling pleased with what I had set up. I'd tested it, capturing myself walking in and out of the house, copying back the backed up images from my machine at work. I felt better, knowing that at least I would have evidence to show Ben if the intruder showed again.

2.

The first person the web cam caught was Karen. I was checking it was working when she called round at the front door. I turned off the screen, not wanting her to feel unnerved at being caught on camera.

I was glad she called around. It was getting dark and I felt uneasy in the cottage. Ben still hadn't called back about the key.

'I was wondering if you'd like to come over for a drink this evening. David's just been to pick up the kids....' She breathed in deeply trying to steady her voice. She looked sad and lost now that she faced several days without George and Sophia.

'Missing them?' I asked, smiling sympathetically.

She nodded, pursing her lips, perhaps trying to stop her tears.

*

We sat on the floor in front of the sofa, leaning our backs against it, our legs out straight warming our feet in front of the stove. She'd opened a bottle of red wine and poured most of it into two large glasses.

'I didn't want George to go,' she said swallowing a mouthful of wine. 'Not so soon after the other day. I'd much rather keep an eye on him here.'

'Has he seemed OK?' I asked concerned.

'Yes, he's been fine. A bit more sleepy and tired may be. But no, he's been good. Thanks to you,' she said smiling and turning to look at me.

I wanted to say that I was sure David would look after him, but I knew their background and I was not sure that he would. I frowned into my glass and watched it coat the sides of the glass while I swirled it round.

'How've you been?' she asked, still smiling at me.

I breathed in deeply, thinking that I would say that I'd been feeling fine. I sighed out. 'Absolutely knackered,' I admitted.

She laughed out loud and grabbed my leg, squeezing it, amused. She removed her hand and took another large mouthful of wine, swilling it appreciatively around her mouth before gulping it down.

'Ah,' she said with pleasure. 'I've missed having a drink,' she said looking longingly at her glass. 'I've been off it while I was taking my meds, and I don't like drinking when the kids are in the house. I'd feel terrible if something happened to them and I wasn't in a state to drive them to get help.' She frowned, distracted, perhaps thinking of the trouble George had been in a couple of days earlier.

I was already feeling the effects of the strong wine. My head felt quite light. I could feel that my cheeks were filling with warmth and I felt my lips turned up in a contented smile. My legs and body tingled pleasantly and I felt the most relaxed I'd been all day.

My phone buzzed beside me on the floor. I picked it up straight away hoping it was a message from Ben. Karen looked towards it, following the noise and then politely turned away so that I could read the message in privacy.

'It's from Ben,' I said openly. 'I was waiting for a message.' He'd found the key. His short message told me that it was where he'd kept it. Hadn't moved it since Jake had given it to him. I switched the phone off and then threw it on top of my jacket on the arm-chair. 'I'm not expecting any other calls this evening,' I said, so that we could relax again.

'You get on well with him, don't you,' she said almost seriously.

I shrugged. I was beginning to feel more at ease again with him. 'He's OK,' I said neutrally. 'No he's nice,' I said wanting to sound more positive. 'He's a good bloke.' I nodded, smiling at my increased warm feelings towards him recently.

'Do you find him a bit too much like Jake?' she asked gently.

I breathed in, a sharp breath at the mention of Jake's name. It wasn't because Karen said his name. I always twitched when anyone mentioned him. I breathed out, taking time to consider my feelings towards him in that way. 'I used to definitely,' I said. 'They look and sound so similar in some ways. But I'm starting to see him more as just Ben, but slowly. It's taken a long time.'

She nodded with understanding.

'And Margaret? Do you still see much of her?' she asked.

I wanted to say 'not if I can possibly avoid it', but I held my breath and my tongue while I thought of a more diplomatic response. 'Not so much as I used to no. She doesn't visit,' I said shrugging as if this should be an issue, and then added, 'although she's hard to avoid in Pennance.' I tensed up, realising that I'd still phrased my response in terms of avoiding her.

'You don't like her do you?' Karen said smiling.

'I can't stand her,' I blurted out laughing. 'Do you know her well?' I asked.

'I used to, but I doubt she's changed,' she said still laughing. 'I find her very,' she searched for the word, 'well just bloody nosy really, to the point of being rude.'

I laughed, glad that Karen felt the same way as I did. 'I find it very disconcerting,' I admitted. 'I'm still not used to everyone knowing who I am.'

'And what you're up to, what you bought at the supermarket, what you had to eat, what ailment you had while you were waiting in the surgery waiting room….' She tailed off raising her eyes, understanding my view.

I smiled at her. I was glad that she felt as I did, but I also felt sorry for her. She must have come under more scrutiny than I did, being from a prominent family in the village. I imagined Jake's mother gossiping about her in the post office, her divorce, her affair.

She got up, pushing herself up from the floor. 'Another drink?' she asked.

As I waited for her to come back with the wine, I thought of Tom Riley again. I didn't understand what he hoped to achieve by breaking into my house and then stealing a T-shirt. It seemed bizarre. Did he just want to frighten me? He certainly had achieved that. That he would break in again while I slept, was my greatest concern. I would bolt the door when I got home. There were two bolts, one on the top and one on the bottom of the door.

I wondered if I would sleep. I pictured myself, sitting up in bed, listening out for anyone approaching the house. Was I being naïve not taking this more seriously? Should I have told Ben? My instinct was not to, although I didn't know why. I looked at Karen as she approached, wondering whether I should ask her opinion as to what to do. I didn't want to spoil her evening though. I didn't want to trouble her with my concerns while she had her own with George away from her.

I felt agitated remembering about the intruder and noticed that I'd became too hot as I fidgeted, the stove and alcohol warming me right through. I stripped off my jumper without thinking, throwing it onto the arm chair with my jacket and phone.

'Christ,' I heard Karen say. I turned round quickly to look up at her to see what was wrong. She looked down with a look of distress pinching her face. Her mouth was open, but unable to speak, as she looked down at my arm. I twitched my gaze down, not realising straight away what had caused her concern.

I only had a T-shirt on and the long scar on my arm was exposed. She knelt down beside me, staring at it and then looked up at me. 'Does it hurt?' she said, horrified at the contorted pink scar that ran down my arm.

'No, no,' I said laughing, wanting to pacify her concern. 'It feels tight if anything. It feels stiff, as if it's not joined up quite right when I move,' I said, wriggling my fingers.

You could see the lines of tendons like spokes running from my fingers to my wrist as I lifted my fingers up and down. The movement continued up from my wrist to where the scar began and then the rest of my forearm heaved unevenly, the scar and damaged tissue moving unnaturally. 'That's quite tiring actually,' I said shaking my hand out and laughing.

She reached forward involuntarily, as if to touch the scar, and looked up for my permission. 'Really it's not sore to touch,' I said.

She tentatively pressed her finger tips onto the ridge of my scar, running them up and down. Her touch felt numb directly on the scar. I'd never got all the feeling back on its surface.

'It's smooth,' she said, almost in awe. She moved her fingers along the edges, where pink-brown seal met the undamaged skin. I could feel her fingers better here, a tingling feeling running up my arm and down my chest from where she ran her fingers. She stretched out her hand, enclosing my forearm in her hand, stroking slowly and firmly up my arm, feeling the shape of it. She smiled, running her hand past my elbow and underneath the sleeve of my T-shirt. She lingered on my muscle at the top of my arm, squeezing it.

'You have nice arms,' she said, admiringly.

I smiled at her compliment, able to accept it under the influence of alcohol. I liked the way she touched me, firm and confident but with soft hands. Her touch made my skin feel alert, not just where she placed her hand but all around it. It tingled craving that she stroke there next.

'They get a bit muscley,' I said, distracting myself from the too pleasurable sensation.

'I like muscley arms,' she said, still stroking up and down, ignoring my complaint.

'I prefer yours,' I said looking at her forearm. 'You have elegant arms.'

I liked her pale skin. I liked the dark freckles that were sprinkled liberally on her arms. You didn't notice them at first, but they were irresistible once you had. I was tempted to reach out with my finger, to trace along every inch of her arm, joining the dots. I put up my hand and held it tentatively just above her skin, feeling only the cushion of warm air and the downy hair on her arm between us.

There was a loud knock at the door. We both twitched, almost lifting off the floor with the fright. My heart fluttered in my chest. I snapped my head round, my eyes staring wide towards the doorway.

Karen got to her feet quickly and walked towards the door. I almost shouted out to her to stop. I worried who it might be. She disappeared from my view into the hallway and I heard the dull sound of her footsteps in the hallway. I could hear that she didn't even hesitate at opening the door. I felt myself starting to panic at who she might be letting into the house.

I heard her voice say something in surprise. She didn't sound frightened, but annoyed. I heard a man's voice, deep so that it carried, but I still couldn't make out the words. I could hear Karen's voice rise slightly, more agitated.

I got up and walked slowly to the door. Karen was speaking faster now, the quick fire of words of an argument. The deeper voice came back, beating an answer back again. I stepped into the hallway, wanting to make my presence known to whoever was threatening her, so that he knew she was not alone.

I recognised her husband immediately. He wore the same kind of unpleasant expression on his face as the one I'd seen that first day. He turned his eyes towards me but didn't say anything. His face rippled with displeasure, his jaw clenching with disapproval.

I saw a sneer catch his nose and the corner of his lips as he turned away in the darkness. Karen turned to me. She looked embarrassed and also a little afraid.

'He's brought George home,' she said upset.

I mouthed the word sorry, regretting that I had appeared. I suspected I only made the situation worse. I stepped out of the hallway and back into the sitting room, listening out at the door, in case his voice became angry.

The tones of their voices remained abrupt, but I couldn't hear what they said. He talked more quietly now he knew Karen had company. I felt nervous standing listening to him, still unnerved by the intruder at the cottage.

I heard the front door shut firmly and Karen walk towards the sitting room. She had tears in her eyes when she came in. She held George in her arms. He looked pale and tired and rested his head on his mother's shoulder.

'David said he wouldn't settle so he's brought him back,' she said. I could hear the brittleness in her voice. Anger and sorrow flickered across her eyes, as she jogged George up and down trying to comfort him.

I opened my mouth looking down at my feet. I was about to say that I should go, so she could comfort George.

'Will you stay?' she said. 'I'd like you to stay tonight if you want to.'

I was relieved that she asked. I was reluctant to step out into the night, knowing David had been there. I feared going back to the cottage alone in the dark.

I realised that I hadn't checked the loft, and now my vivid imagination was inventing every kind of horrible scenario from that omission.

3.

I almost lived at the house those few days over Christmas. I would go for a short walk when I got up in the morning; I was still too tired to run. I showered at the cottage, changing into fresh clothes and went back to Karen's around lunch time.

I would play with George while Karen prepared large roast lunches and then all three of us would watch cartoon films in the afternoons. Sometimes Karen and I would have time alone in the evenings but she didn't drink now George was home.

I slept on the sofa, warm and content by the stove. Karen would kiss me good night before she went upstairs, pressing her soft closed lips against mine, letting them stay pressed into mine for a few seconds, her eyes closed. If she had opened her lips, closing them moistly around mine, with a different intention, I wouldn't have drawn away.

She gave me a new jacket as a Christmas present, to replace the one I had lost in the water. It was an expensive one, much better than the one I'd lost. I blushed at her generosity. I bought George a new dinosaur, a pterodactyl. He ran around the house with it, his arm lifted high, flying it through the air. It was the happiest time I'd had in years, waking up each morning in a warm house of people I cared for.

Sophia was back New Year's Eve and I returned to the cottage. It seemed colder and more empty after staying at Karen's. I didn't feel too vulnerable during the day. I kept the front door bolted. I could see the surroundings of the house quite clearly in the sunlight that beamed through the trees.

I was dreading the dark though, dreading night falling and impenetrable darkness drawing tight around the cottage giving me no warning of anyone's approach. I cycled slowly up to Pennance late afternoon, getting some last minute-shopping before the store closed for New Year. It was starting to get dark so I grabbed a couple of tins of soup, some chocolate and noodles, my imagination failing me again. I was unchaining my bike when Ben passed by on his way to the pub.

'Do you fancy a drink?' he said jovially.

'Starting early,' I said laughing and raising an eyebrow.

'Haven't had New Years off for ages. Taking full advantage of it,' he said grinning. 'You coming in then?' he said beckoning in the direction of the pub.

'No I want to get back before it gets dark,' I said, pursing my lips together in an embarrassed smile.

He frowned at me, looking concerned. 'What's the problem?' he asked.

'I just don't feel that happy about getting home in the dark,' I said evasively.

He looked at me considering for a moment. I wondered if he still thought me paranoid.

'You should really have a look at that house up near mine,' he said. 'It's still up for sale you know, but it won't be for long. It's a nice house.'

I shook my head, not wanting to have that conversation again. 'I'm just feeling a bit cowardly today. I've been staying at Karen's so I'm just a bit jittery about going back to an empty cottage tonight.' I said smiling.

'But, I want to get a move on now.' I said, pushing on my bike, ready to go.

He still frowned at me. 'How about I walk you home?' he said seriously. 'Come and have a drink, and then I'll walk you home, check under your bed, make sure you're all right. How about that?' he said trying to smile again. 'And if you have any worries in the night, you can call me. I can be there in seconds. There's no need to bother Karen.'

I was tempted to be annoyed with him again, but he was right, it would be better to call him and not bother Karen now Sophia was home.

I relented, nodding.

'Great. Now come and have a pint,' he said, happy.

I only stayed for one drink. I didn't want to feel its effect too much. I wanted to be alert while I was alone in the cottage. Ben managed to drink three times as much in the same time and was quite buoyant by the time I wanted to leave. But he walked home with me as he'd promised, after pleading with me to stay longer several times. He looked around the house quite thoroughly, taking a torch outside to check around the back of the house.

He stood in the doorway, about to leave.

'If it's Tom you're worried about, I wouldn't,' he said. 'Not tonight anyway,'

I looked at him not understanding.

'Saw him heading home this afternoon when I was at mum's. He lives at the end cottage. Had a huge bottle of vodka with him. He ain't going nowhere believe me. He already looked in quite a state as it was.'

I nodded and frowned, not comforted by his observation.

'Come on now,' he said smiling, his eyes refocusing on mine a fraction too slowly, dulled by the alcohol. 'Give us a little smile,' he said grinning stupidly.

I laughed reluctantly.

'That's better. Any problem at all, you ring me. Me and several other big blokes will be down here in a flash. All right?' he said, trying to reassure me.

I nodded, just to appease him.

'Oh, I'm in town first day back at work,' he said slowly remembering something, pointing an uncoordinated bent forefinger in the air. 'You in the office? I was wondering if you'd like a bite to eat after work?'

'Yeah,' I said placidly. 'What do you fancy?' I said.

'How about I book somewhere for us?' he said. 'I'll surprise you.'

'OK,' I said shrugging.

'Right,' he said. 'Another pint's waiting for me.' He said, stepping out of the door. 'Good night then,' He leaned forward, to put his arms around me and bent his head as if to kiss me. I flinched, flustered by his drunken over-familiarity.

'Come on,' he said smiling. 'It's New Year's Eve,' he spread his arms wide as if he was not asking for anything unreasonable. He stumbled to the side, shining the torch around the undergrowth and bent down pulling something from the bank. 'Right, pretend this is mistletoe then,' he said holding up a gnarled piece of ivy.

I looked up at it, and then raised an eyebrow at Ben. He looked like he was not going to leave until he'd had his New Year's Eve kiss.

'All right then,' I said, leaning up on tip toes to reach his lips. He pressed his face into mine, our lips not quite coinciding. I had to stiffen my neck, as he pushed his face down too hard. It felt unpleasant after Karen's goodnight kisses. His skin was tougher, not like the smooth, pliable skin of Karen's delicious cheek. His short bristles pricked my skin as the flesh around his lips pushed into my face. He smelled strong, male, and his breath was sour from the bitter that he had drunk.

He pulled away, licking his lips. 'See,' he said his eyes drooping a little, 'not so bad was it?'

*

I still didn't feel at ease in the house. I went to bed early and jammed a shirt in the gap under the door, stopping it from being opened by anyone from the landing. I did not turn the radio on. I wanted to be able to hear the creaks and groans the cottage made, listening out for any anomalous sound. I lay in bed fully clothed, mentally ready to open the bedroom window and leap out into the lane if I needed to.

I switched off my bedroom light around 1 o'clock in the morning, daring myself to get some sleep. It was lighter than I expected. The moon was not quite full, but reflected a white cold light down into the wood and through my bedroom window, making the bedroom surfaces appear leaden.

I leaned up in bed and looked out of the window into the lane. I could only see detail from the corners of my eyes, only being able to make out shapes if I looked at them obliquely. I saw no movement outside as I stared with wide eyes out of the window. I lay back down and stared at the silvery ceiling above me, half afraid that, if I fell asleep, I might never wake up again.

I woke to bright sunshine beaming hazily into the room, warming the dust and wafting particles into the air that glistened in the sunlight. I felt a wave of fear clench my chest, worrying too late that I had fallen asleep, followed by cleansing relief that I was still alive, that no-one had broken into the house in the night.

I felt more confident having spent a night there without incident. I began to relax more the next day. It was a beautiful crisp morning and I went for a walk along the coast. I saw Karen in the kitchen through the window on the way back, laying out lunch in front of the kids. I waved as I walked past and I saw her smile and wave back.

I went to bed early again, it may have been as early as eight o'clock. I listened to the radio this time, promising myself that I would be all right if I switched it off before twelve o'clock. I thought that anything bad would happen after midnight. I had no reason to think this. It was just a rule that my mind had made up, in the absence of any company to tell me otherwise.

I drifted off well before twelve and woke once sometime in the early hours of the morning, switching off the world service and quickly falling asleep again. I think I'd had at least ten hours sleep by the time I woke up to the sound of my alarm clock.

I showered quickly and dressed in some thick cycling trousers and a fleece top. I would get warm cycling to work, but the air would be icy when I free-wheeled down the hills. I didn't bother with breakfast, just sipping a mug of instant coffee as I got my things ready.

I hurriedly opened the front door, wanting to get on my way earlier than usual. I almost didn't notice the parcel outside. I kicked it with my foot as I strode out of the door, single minded and fixed on getting to my bike. The parcel was quite light, scraping across the dried mud and stones in front of the step, at the force of my gentle kick.

I looked down at it. I was confused that I hadn't heard the postman and I was also surprised that he'd been so early. Then I noticed that there was no stamp, not even an address on the parcel. I assumed I'd missed someone while I'd been in the shower, and picked up the package and brought it inside to put on the table.

I didn't receive many parcels, especially unexpected ones. I ran my fingernail down the centre of the lid, slitting open the thin brown tape and prising the flaps open. There was no further wrapping.

Inside laid a rag doll. She was made of hessian, with coarse brown skin, and had yellow strands of woollen hair. The doll or the box smelled. A pocket of acrid and charred air reached my nose as I pulled the doll from the box. The hair at the back had been burned off. The wool crumbled in my fingers where I held the doll's head. I turned her over to see her injured scalp and saw the back of her body had been slashed and red paint squeezed into the slits. I turned her over in my hands, incredulous at what I held. If I'd had any doubt about what the doll represented, the fact that she wore my missing T-shirt would have made the message clear.

4.

I didn't react how I thought I would. I was so surprised by what someone had done to scare me, the distaste of it, that I felt fury burn right through me. I had no doubt who had done this. I threw the doll in my rucksack, locked the front door, and set off towards Pennance.

I hardly noticed the cycle ride up to the village. The anger and adrenaline fuelled my muscles and powered me up to the centre. I didn't hesitate when I reached the green. I turned up the road towards Margaret's house, red-faced with anger and exertion. I passed her cottage and cycled to the end of the row, to Tom Riley's house.

I took the bottom of my fist to the door, pounding it loudly. There was no response at first but I could see the downstairs light was on. I stepped forward again and hammered on the door, wide-eyed with anger.

He opened the door slowly. He was wearing a T-shirt, boxer shorts and a dressing gown loose around his shoulders. Stale air rushed out towards me, moist and heavy with the smell of cigarettes and alcohol. I grimaced involuntarily and looked away with distaste while the fumes passed.

I snapped my gaze back to his face as soon as I could breathe again. 'What the fuck is this about?' I said holding up the doll and shaking it vigorously in front of his face.

He stared at it stupidly, raising his eyebrows to focus his eyes, his mouth hanging open wordlessly.

'What the fuck do you hope to gain by this?' I shouted at him. I glared at him, waiting for him to reply. He didn't respond.

'There's nothing I can do about this bloody case you know. It's not me that's pushing it. I would have settled way back, if not dropped the bloody thing altogether.' I stepped forward, trying to force a response out of him.

He gulped and breathed out. 'I know,' he said in a mangled sleepy way.

I stepped back again repelled by him. 'You're drunk,' I said disgusted at his state. He must have been drinking all night. I didn't know what to say then. I doubted that he understood what I said and why I had called round.

'Why send this then?' I said, still furious but tempering my mood so that I could communicate with him.

He stared at it, pushing his head forward and then back, widening his eyes trying to focus on it. He looked stupid, grotesque. He stared at it clueless, and then he shrugged his shoulders, pushing his bottom lip out like a fat pink slug embedded in his greasy beard.

His nonchalance sparked another explosion of fury in me.

'Well it's really fucking cruel and really fucking juvenile,' I screamed at him, pressing the doll roughly into his chest. He stumbled back, almost falling over, I'd pushed him so hard. He scraped at the side of the wall, grabbing the handrail at the bottom of the stairs to hold himself up.

He looked surprised at me. He looked at me like a kicked dog, dumb, not knowing what it had done wrong. The doll lay on the floor between us. He picked it up and looked at it. Slowly turning it over, looking at it from every angle.

He looked up at me and swallowed again. His eyes were red and sore and watered profusely. 'I don't know what this is,' he slurred.

'Like hell you do,' I shouted at him, still glaring at him.

He looked down at it again, and then pointed to it with his other hand, his yellow-brown stained index finger touching the doll. 'I've never, ever, seen this in my life.' He looked at me, his expression still stupidly innocent. Clueless, he stretched out his arm, offering the doll back to me.

'Keep it,' I snapped at him.

I wasn't going to get any sense out of him. I turned exasperated and still enraged by what he had done. Stupid bastard could have done it when he was drunk last night, I thought. He might not even remember it now, a good bottle of vodka later. Trembling and pulsing with anger, I cycled out of the village.

*

I was still shaking when I got to work. The adrenaline and anger had gone from my body. I shook now that its energy had gone and trembled at the thought of what I had done. It had been stupid confronting Tom like that. If he had been sober or even freshly drunk, I don't know what he might have done. I broke into a sweat thinking about it, regretting my outburst.

I went to the ladies and sat on the loo, breathing in deeply, exhaling in nervous punctuated rasping breaths. I felt nauseous. I felt sick at the danger I had put myself in and at the hate that must have gone into making the doll. I gulped down the sorrow, feeling devastated that someone could be that personally vindictive against me. He must have oozed malevolence as he tore into that doll and charred its hair, soaking the gashes in what he saw as my blood.

A quiet choking cry escaped my throat before I could swallow it down. I desperately wiped my eyes, not wanting them to swell and become pink while I was at work. I started to force myself to breathe in and out again, large calming breaths.

I'd left the only evidence I had with the perpetrator, I realised. I had given the bloody doll back to Tom. I laughed, a breathy short laugh, and shook my head, incredulous at how stupid I'd been. I could have shown the doll to Ben this evening, could have taken it to the police. I had nothing to persuade them with, nothing that couldn't be put down to my paranoia.

'Shit!' I stamped my foot on the floor. 'Shit!' I shouted louder, banging the cubicle wall with my fist.

I cleaned my face in the sink, wiping away the tears with cool water and tissues. I applied some more eyeliner that smeared a little, but I didn't look too bad. I could look as if I was just tired, not as if I had been crying, I persuaded myself, and then I went to my desk.

I stared at my computer screen smiling. In my anger I had forgotten about the web cam. I quickly opened up the backup folder and copied across the images that had been saved since eight o'clock the previous evening.

I loaded them up to play them, fast forwarding through the images. I saw myself walking around the house, stilted and appearing by the front door in the kitchen and then suddenly large right under the doorway to the sitting room. I jerked to the bottom of the stairs and then the image went grey and fuzzy. I must have switched all the lights off downstairs.

I paused the images and opened up a single blank photo. I enlarged a part of it to see if it had any definition. All I saw was grey noise. I swore and dragged the bar of the player along to later in the sequence. It only became light around half seven and it was nearly eight by the time there was enough light to see any detail.

I sat back in my chair, deflated and defeated. I should have kept the kitchen light on. I kicked myself for not thinking that through. If I had kept the light on I would have been able to capture anyone who came close to the house and anyone who broke in. I still had no evidence to give Ben.

5.

I was glad I was seeing Ben that evening. I'd decided that I would tell him everything despite not having any physical evidence to give him. At least I was sure that my persecution was not just an element of my paranoia and guilt.

I hadn't been to the restaurant before and I was running late by the time I found it. I stood outside for a minute, wondering if I had found the right place. I looked at the crisp white menu behind the shining brass-framed glass. It was a small menu of classic meat and fish dishes, priced accordingly. A meal would cost more than I spent on food in a month.

I looked through the window. The tables were generously spaced and covered with stiff white table cloths. I watched a middle-aged couple being escorted to their table. The man was dressed in a jacket and tie and his wife wore a red blazer over a long woollen dress. She clutched at her necklace as she sat down. The waiter did not have a scruffy small note pad. He took their request for drinks, keeping his hands neatly crossed in front of him.

It wasn't the kind of place I usually ate and not the kind of place I'd expected to meet Ben. I stepped inside the front door and walked towards the reception desk. A man in a spotless black jacket raised his eyes to look at me.

'Hi, sorry, I'm not sure if I'm at the right restaurant,' I said feeling out of place. I was wearing jeans, walking shoes and a long waterproof coat. 'I might be meeting someone here. They made the booking.'

'What name's the reservation under madam?' he asked pleasantly.

'Arundell? Ben Arundell?'

He ran his finger down a neatly completed booking page and came to a halt half way down.

'Yes, you've come to the right place. The gentleman's here already I believe.' He lifted his arm, gesturing with an open hand to follow a waiter who stood at the entrance to the main room. 'If you'd like to follow…'

'Is it OK if I go in like this?' I said, pinching my jeans, embarrassed at how inappropriate I looked.

'Of course,' he said neutrally. 'Would you like to leave your rain coat here?'

I felt uncomfortable as I was led to the table, my walking boots clunking noisily on the parquet floor. Ben was at the back of the restaurant on a quiet table in the corner. I had to walk the length of the restaurant, people turning to see what was disturbing their elegant evening as I walked past.

Ben stood up as I approached. He was wearing a smart jumper and jacket. He had his polished brogues on. He looked nervous. He pulled out the chair on the opposite side of the table helping me to sit down. I felt stupid, a helpless woman being aided to sit down on a comfortable chair in my well-worn jeans and walking boots that I had walked hundreds of rugged miles in.

I fidgeted with my fleece top. I was too hot but I only had a T-shirt on underneath and I didn't want to expose my scars. I was feeling too self-conscious already. The waiter gave me the menu and a friendly smile. 'Can I get you anything to drink while you look at the menu?' he asked.

'A glass of champagne I think,' said Ben, answering for me, 'and another for me please.'

I nodded, not wanting to draw any more attention when the waiter looked at me for confirmation. 'And a glass of tap water please,' I said. I had become sweaty and thirsty on the way here, jogging the last couple of hundred yards.

'Bring a bottle of mineral water in fact,' Ben corrected.

The waiter left and Ben turned to me, smiling nervously.

'It's quite expensive here,' I said. 'I wish you'd warned me.' I looked at him upset. I didn't like dressing up particularly, but I didn't like looking foolish.

'No worries about that,' he said smiling. 'It's my shout tonight. Don't worry about the price.'

'It's not that,' I said. I left the words hanging. I wasn't sure he would understand if I explained. I suppose he categorised me as a sporty outdoors girl so why would I want to wear anything else.

The waiter returned with two tall glasses of champagne placing one each in front of us. He turned sensing that we were not ready to order.

'Cheers,' Ben said lightly, lifting his glass.

I reached for my glass, pinching the stem in my fingers, but just twisted it on the white table cloth that stayed perfectly stiff and flat beneath it.

'What are we celebrating?' I asked, looking at him straight in the eye.

'Nothing,' he said blankly. 'Do we have to be celebrating to have a glass of champagne?' he said light-heartedly.

I didn't say anything and took a sip, sharp yeasty bubbles leaping and bursting into my nostrils.

I looked around the room. It was evenly populated. A couple every other table, the bookings staggered not to put too much of a rush on the exclusive kitchen. It was not a family restaurant and it wasn't the kind of place you went out with friends.

'Are we on a date Ben?' I said frowning.

He looked worried, his eyebrows raised and his mouth open a little. He didn't manage to vocalise whatever terrified thought he had in his head.

'I wish you'd told me,' I said, my annoyance starting to affect my voice. I'd had a stressful day and this was an unwelcome distraction.

He frowned then, and looked affronted. 'Well, I thought it would be obvious,' he said sharply. He drew his glass in towards him on the table, twirling it nervously.

'Why? How?' I said in disbelief.

'We've been out together?' He continued when I looked unconvinced. 'We've been getting on well, and I just thought I would take it a step further.' He looked hurt that I wasn't on the same wavelength.

I looked away feeling uncomfortable. I didn't know what to say.

'Well what's wrong with being on a date now you're here,' he said looking pleased to have thought of this saving ploy.

I shook my head. 'Ben I can't,' I said imploring him to stop.

He looked at me thinking, his eyes flicking intently between mine. He looked down at the table. 'I know it's only been just over a year, since Jake,' he broke off. 'But we can take it slow,' he said. 'I don't mind that at all.'

'Ben, please,' I said. 'I can't see you, not in that way. I'm flattered,' I said trying to soften any disappointment, 'but I can't think of you that way.'

'You seemed to think of me in that way a few months ago,' he said with a slight edge to his voice.

I blushed, remembering that evening, feeling nauseous at the image of Ben on top of me, his trousers around his ankles. I gulped and hesitated. I didn't want to say anything too cruel, but I didn't want to encourage him.

'That was once only,' I said quietly. 'We shouldn't have done that.'

He was silent for a moment looking hurt and awkward. 'But in time,' he said sounding more desperate. 'We get on. That's the most important thing isn't it? Love comes slow for some couples,' he said looking hopeful at me.

I felt sick. If I hadn't loved Jake enough then my love for Ben would be more deficient. 'It's not enough Ben,' I said shaking my head.

He reached across the table, taking my hand in his, trapping it between his palms. I felt repulsion ripple up my arm, making my whole body want to shrink and curl inwards to get away from him.

'Just spend some time with me. I don't mean at the pub. Let's do this kind of thing more often. Go for a walk.

Have some days out together.' He said it all softly, imploring, begging.

I didn't know what to do. I didn't know what I could say to persuade him that I couldn't be with him.

'Perhaps we could go on holiday together. We'd have separate bedrooms and that. Just be nice to get away and spend some time together. We could go up to Scotland on the train. Go walking in the highlands. Or go to France on Eurostar.' He started to look away, becoming carried away with his thoughts.

I tugged my hand away from his, taking advantage of his distraction. I looked at him, unblinking.

'Ben. No,' I said.

He looked shocked. I had got through to him, and it had hurt. He sat back in his chair, looking deflated, no more optimistic imploring words to say to me. He looked embarrassed, looking away across the restaurant, taking sips from his glass.

I awkwardly sipped from my glass while I wondered what to do. It would embarrass him even more if I left now, the noisy woman in her boots conspicuously leaving her date behind. I didn't want to hurt or humiliate him. I was sorry that he felt that way. And I needed him as a friend.

I cleared my throat and picked up the menu. 'Shall we order something to eat?' I said quietly.

'This is because of Karen isn't it?' he said still looking away. His eyes had drifted wide open as he'd thought and they looked angry and glazed. He turned to look at me, expecting me to answer.

'I know you've been seeing her almost every day,' he said accusingly.

'What does that have to do with anything?' I said confused.

'Well who sees their neighbours that often? Especially a townie like you. Who stays at their neighbour's house when their own bed is a hundred metres away? Who throws themselves down a cliff to save their neighbour's bloody child?' his voice had started to rise as he shot the accusations at me.

'I'm not going to deny that I'm very fond of Karen and that I spend time with her,' I said annoyed.

I thought I had rationally answered his questions. He fell silent for a moment. He glared at me, his anger still making his neck pulse.

'Are you sleeping with her?' he said plainly.

'What the?' I was taken aback by his blatant and intrusive question. 'No.' I said neutrally. 'No, I am not.'

'Well what is it then?' he said still angry. 'I don't understand the spell that woman has on people,' he said shaking his head. 'She's wound you round her little finger. The Trevithicks were all like that. Can't do enough for them,' he spat. 'And it just seems a bit sick that she's done the same to you. Really just a bit sick.'

'She's been very kind to me,' I said defending her, not confident that I understood what Ben was implying.

He looked at me annoyed. I could feel that my face had dropped, my expression betraying my lack of understanding. He sat back in his chair again, pushing himself away with his hand on the table. He looked smug, pleased with himself.

'She hasn't told you, has she?' he said proudly.

'I don't know what you're talking about,' I said irritable at his conceit. 'We've talked about lots of things.'

'She hasn't told you this though has she,' he said laughing.

I didn't say anything. I didn't want to play a hurtful guessing game with him.

'She was Jake's girlfriend,' he said smiling nastily. 'Love of his life,' he said emphasising each word. 'He was going to marry her, that's how much he loved her. He didn't marry you did he, but he would have married her. She broke his heart when she left school and went away to university. I'm not surprised she didn't mention it, come to think of it.' He took a satisfied glug of the last of his champagne.

I felt faint and cold. It was an odd omission. We had told each other so many personal and secret things, things that I had never told anyone else. I'd found her so open right from the start.

It wasn't like taking a powerful blow, one that knocks you out. It was more like someone had tugged me, making me stumble. I felt unbalanced, not sure of the world now. I felt as if there was something wrong, but I didn't quite know what.

'I could love you though.' Ben was talking. I hadn't taken in the first words he'd said. He was speaking softly again, imploring again, reaching across the table, clawing at me with apologetic hands.

I looked at him incredulous. What would make him stop? Was there nothing I could say to him to stop him pawing me? What would he do to try to persuade me to be with him? What lengths would he go to?

I stood up quickly, scraping the chair noisily across the floor. I felt dizzy. Was he telling the truth about Karen? Could I trust him any more? What else had he done to try and turn me away from Karen and encourage me? Had he been the one trying to scare me out of my home, so that I would move closer to him? He had a key. He'd known when I was out of the house.

I couldn't speak. I stared at him genuinely afraid.

6.

I sat on a bench on the platform waiting for the train. My stomach felt empty and nauseous, and I shook with anger and fear. I'd left the restaurant without another word to Ben. I didn't tell him what I thought, what I suspected about him. I didn't want to hear anything that he might say in reply. It made me feel ill, the pleasure he had taken in telling me how little Jake had loved me. It had not affected me in the way he expected it to. It hadn't been a crushing revelation to me. But that Ben would try to hurt me by undermining the relationship I had with my dead partner, who died in such a violent way, I thought terrifyingly revealing.

I thought it hurtful, manipulative. It showed a worrying lack of self-control, the same lack of control he showed when he slept with me. My whole body shuddered again at the memory, my skin writhing with discomfort. I remembered the rough kiss he had given me on New Year's Eve, how he had no idea how unpleasant I might find it. My lips curled up in disgust as if with an unpleasant taste. I wished I could wash my mouth out, wished I could clean away the unpleasant memory.

Could he have broken in, I thought again. He certainly had the opportunity. He was the only person I knew who had a key to my home. Could I see him preparing the doll, hacking away at it in anger? I could imagine him with the contorted sneering face that I had seen tonight, preparing the evocative representation of me, knowing it would affect me. Who else knew me so intimately to make that accurate a model of me?

Did Tom know about the scars on my back? I shook my head. It was possible. I remembered that Ben had told me that he was one of the part-timers at the fire service. Anyone who'd attended the accident that night might have told him what happened. They could have described the trapped charred body of the popular local policeman and his shredded partner who survived. In fact, it was possible the whole village might know the shape of my scars, may be privy to the details of my injuries. Such delicious details would have been quickly passed around.

I was starting to panic. The list of people I distrusted suddenly expanded to the entire village. The pressure from my anxiety was making my head ache and my shoulders trembled as I tensed them tighter. I closed my eyes and breathed in deeply, trying to stop myself from spiralling into despair and distraction. I couldn't black out at the station, go into a numb trance. I needed to keep control of myself.

I needed to talk to someone. I needed someone to pick out the rational concrete pieces and put them together coherently for me. I rubbed my forehead trying to force my head to think clearly. I felt disoriented. I didn't know who I could trust. The only person near to me who I would have approached was Karen, but my train of thought stumbled when I pictured her. I felt hurt that she hadn't told me about Jake, that she had been the most significant woman in his life. Her omission stopped me trusting her completely. I felt less eager to run to her and spill out my fears making myself completely open and vulnerable to her.

The train approached, squealing to a halt slowly by the platform. I stared at it unfocused, my body and mind paralysed by my fears and suspicions. I saw dark shapes of people out of the corners of my eyes getting on and off the train, a blur of a late-comer running across the platform and jumping into the train. I saw a man in uniform twist and turn looking down the platform and then heard the whistle giving the train permission to leave. I saw the horizontal shape move and slide, and then the far wall of the train station flash into view again.

*

I stayed at a hotel near the station. I could barely speak when I checked in. It was the right thing to do, what I would have done if I was thinking rationally. It was the safest place for me and I managed to sleep for several hours. I was thinking more clearly in the morning and got an early train home.

I spent the journey ringing locksmiths until I found one who was available that day to replace the door lock and fix locks to all the windows.

I had a text from Ben. He apologised and asked if we could meet up. I replied straight away telling him to leave me alone. I willed the train on, wanting to get home and get the locks changed.

I circled the cottage when I got back, trying to look through all the windows, checking that no-one was in the house. I took a deep breath opening the front door and once again dashed round the house in a burst of adrenaline checking that no-one was there. I quickly covered the main rooms and stood staring at the covered loft hatch.

I pushed up the ladder against the wall and climbed up reaching out a hand to push up the hatch door. I felt vulnerable climbing up into the room, my head first. It felt cold and exposed as I stepped up into the darkness. I put out my arm into the clinging air and felt around the sloping ceiling for the light switch, my desperate scraping fingers betraying my fear. The light revealed everything in an instant. Grey cardboard boxes, an old lampshade, a book shelf there wasn't room for. No intruders.

I looked down and saw the red shoebox. I hadn't touched it since that day I peeked inside while Jake was out. I felt guilty, sliding it over and opening the lid. It still felt like Jake's secret past.

There he was again, on top of the pile, walking in the mountains. He looked peculiarly flat and two dimensional. It was difficult to imagine him as a solid person when I looked at the image. It was difficult to flesh him out.

I slowly and hesitantly pushed my fingers down the side of the pile of photos, feeling the thick edges of the images flick past my finger tips. It was right at the bottom. I could feel the smooth mounting of the formal picture. I curled my nails then finger tips beneath it, tipping the rest of the pile to the side. I drew it out slowly, the group appearing one by one, until I saw Jake and then his adorable companion.

I felt a peculiar mix of sadness and pride. I was sad or perhaps disappointed to recognise Karen's young face, but my heart filled in admiration at how beautiful she looked. I think I smiled at her image with fondness. She didn't look much different to how she did now. She just had the plumpness of teenage puppy fat. Perhaps it only struck me at that moment how attractive I found her.

I felt no jealousy that she had taken Jake's heart. I felt no envy that she had been the love of his life. If anything, I felt jealous that he had been with her, repelled by the thought of Jake touching her elegant pale body.

I wanted him to remove his hands from hers in the photo. I wanted him to leave her alone. I dropped the photo back onto the pile and quickly hid it, closing the box with its lid.

I stepped back down the ladder and stood in the sitting room feeling deflated. Ben had been telling the truth at least about Karen. I felt dejected, this thorn of information sitting uncomfortably.

7.

I didn't stay long in the cottage. My discomfort and agitation soon had me walking down the lane towards the manor house. The children were both still at home so I approached the house slowly, trying to see if they were up. I didn't want to face Sophia or see George in my emotional state.

I could see Karen through the kitchen window, laying out the table. She was still wearing her dressing gown, tied loosely around her waist. I could see her pale chest, bare and descending beneath the towelling folds. She was concentrating, looking down, dealing out the plates. No-one disturbed her, grabbing her attention, making her twist in every direction. She looked sad and drawn this morning. It made my chest feel heavier seeing her like that.

She looked up, looking right into my eyes. It made me stop and stare at her, feeling embarrassed of my emotional state. I felt like I was intruding approaching the house without invitation. I wondered if I should keep walking, pretend I was going for a stroll. I didn't want to admit and expose to her my feelings that had been rattled by her secret. She tried to smile, pulling her lips up, but her eyes looked sad and resigned. She turned away from me in the direction of the hallway and I walked up the steps to the front door.

I could see that her eyes looked tired and slightly swollen when she opened the door. I didn't want to ask. I felt uncomfortable asking after her with the secret still not cleared between us. I didn't feel close enough to her at that moment.

'Come in,' she whispered, again attempting a sad smile.

I came in silently and watched her carefully close the door.

'They're still asleep,' she whispered, 'Late night.'

She turned away from me and led into the kitchen, her bare feet scuffing the tiled floor.

'Shut the door,' she said.

I pushed it behind me, letting it slowly and quietly click to.

She turned around and looked at me. I didn't move. I could feel the emotion stretching the back of my mouth. I didn't know what I wanted to say to her or what would make me feel better. I didn't know what she could say to resolve the issue.

'Would you like a drink?' she said. She tipped her head to the side and smiled at me properly, perhaps seeing my discomfort. Her eyes creased into the smile but looked like they may cry.

I nodded still unable to find the right words to say to her.

She turned around and filled the kettle, carefully getting out the crockery, trying not to make too much noise.

I shuffled nervously and strode around the table and towards the window. I looked through the glass but didn't see anything. My mind was fully occupied with trying to form the words to bring up the subject. I didn't want to look foolish or start saying something that would make me burst into tears or make her feel bad.

I breathed in deeply and then blew out a long noisy breath trying to keep control, letting the constant flowing noise fill me with calm.

'You were out last night,' she said, not as a question. 'I called round late. I don't think you were in,'

I didn't turn round to face her. 'Yes,' I said, my voice squeezing over a lump in my throat. 'I, I stayed the night in Plymouth,' I said briefly, not wanting to talk about the evening with Ben. I wanted to ask her plainly about Jake. I didn't want to ask her as a result of Ben's nasty gossip.

She was silent again. I heard the kettle bubble and steam and click off. I didn't hear her move though. I expected the sound of a teapot being pulled along the surface towards the kettle and the pouring of water hitting the bottom of the pot.

'I hear you were on a date with Ben?' She tried to say it lightly, as if she was pleased and interested to hear about a romantic episode in my life. But her voice cracked and rose over the words.

I stood with my heart thumping in my chest. I could feel the strong pulse in my throat, hear it my ears. My eyes opened wide in surprise and hope. I had to keep swallowing to keep the lump at the back of my mouth from constricting my throat. I turned round, seeing her face for a moment before she turned around protecting herself.

She'd looked devastated. I'd glimpsed her eyes raised in pain, her mouth twitching down about to descend fully into grief, desperately trying to control her voice that was giving away her sorrow with every word.

She lifted her hand up to her face. She must have been wiping away a tear. She was breathing quickly and sniffing and looking around in front of her, uncomfortable and upset.

My face started to smile, cautiously hoping at what it meant. I stepped towards her, started saying her name.

'Are you seeing Ben?' she said quickly. Her voice wobbled with little control.

I stepped forward again. I was standing just a few centimetres behind her. She was wiping her face roughly with her right hand, her left twitching beside her body. I started to reach out my hand, wanting to touch and console her agitated hand.

'Are you?' she said more loudly, more upset.

'No, no, I'm not seeing Ben,' I said. I couldn't stop myself from smiling, even though my voice was full of compassion.

I put my hand forward, reaching out to her. I could feel the warmth of her hand before I touched it, the skin on my hand prickling with eagerness to touch her. I slipped my fingers over hers, gulping at the touch and feelings it sent through me. She squeezed her hand, tightening our interlocking fingers together.

She lifted her hand to her chest, pulling mine with it, drawing me closer to her for comfort. I felt her chest heave with emotion beneath my hand, quick at first but then starting to slow and calm as we stood together. I was standing rigid behind her not knowing or daring what to expect. I started to relax, letting my body fall closer to hers.

My breasts lightly touched her back, the front of my body instantly becoming alert waiting for the next sensual touch. The sensation made me breathe out sharply. I know she heard it. Her deep, heavy-hearted breathing had stopped. She lifted her head, holding it rigid, listening to me and how I reacted.

I pushed forward, out bodies sealing slowly and gently together. I breathed more quickly as she shuffled her weight on to her other foot, her buttocks stroking past my groin, teasing me. I lifted up my free hand and gently scooped her hair away from her pale neck. She tilted her head away, exposing more of her skin.

I could smell her. I could smell her hair and her warm skin. It filled my head as I leaned forward to press my lips onto her shoulder. She was holding her breath, waiting for my lips to come into contact with her. I opened my mouth slightly, and gently kissed at her hairline. She breathed out sharply.

I was almost scared at her reaction, scared at what I was doing to her. I kissed her again, more moistly, taking more of her into my mouth. She moaned this time, the sound of her reaction making me twinge between my legs.

It was addictive, kissing her, feeling and hearing her reaction. I reached round with my hand wanting to hold her. It slipped between the folds of her dressing gown finding the naked warm skin of her stomach. I stopped, almost shocked at finding and touching her, worrying if she wanted me to go this far.

She squeezed my hand at her chest. She pulled it down slowly opening up the top of her dressing gown and pressing it gently onto her breast. I gasped as my palm stroked over her nipple, standing out alert to my touch. Her hand twitched again, encouraging my movements. I gently started to squeeze her breast, in small circling movements while I let my other hand drift lower down her belly, tracing her skin with my finger tips from side to side.

My hand brushed past the top of her hair. Again I felt unsure whether she wanted me to go this far. She squeezed my hand at her breast again and squirmed trying to move my hand that hovered tantalisingly at her hair.

I ran my fingers lower and lower, feeling her tense with every pass closer. I hesitated at the top of her lips, swallowing and feeling fuzzy with arousal as my finger tips felt the warm, moist hair between her legs.

I pressed my fingers lower. I let them hover, gently parting the hair, and then slid my finger slowly between her wet lips. She tensed up, leaning forward pulling me closer into her. I started to circle her slowly, pulling her into me with the rest of my hand. She squeezed my hand hard over her breast in time with my movements. She breathed out sharply with each stroke. I breathed out with her, finding her arousal overwhelming.

I moved quicker, touching her with all my fingers, feeling her get bigger and swollen. She was soaking wet and I could smell her moisture, warm and narcotic as it rose up to me. I could feel her start to tense as I stroked her round and round. I heard her breathing quicker and quicker, could feel her peak under my fingers. I squeezed her tight as I felt her come, holding her upright, letting her enjoy every pleasurable contraction. She pulsed beneath me, holding her breath to silence herself as her body shook.

We breathed together as she came down. I almost felt the same relief as her from her tension. She turned around slowly holding my wet hand, rolling her soft face across mine until our lips touched. She licked her lips moistening our kiss, succulently stroking her lips across mine. I felt our bodies seal again, her breasts moulding into mine, her thigh pressing up between my legs.

She heard a noise from upstairs and stepped back abruptly from me. I think my head was too filled with lust to have heard it. I heard the steps down the stairs though. My arousal drained away, leaving me cold.

Karen swept her dressing gown in front of her, tightening up the belt, and turned her back to me. She switched the kettle back on and noisily rearranged the cups in front of her. I stood there stupidly, my brain numb, my eyes wide when Sophia opened the kitchen door.

She looked at me with that expression that looked like it could spontaneously change to any other. She said nothing and turned her gaze on her mother's back, watching what she did, analysing her behaviour.

She turned her attention back to me but talked to her mother. 'I thought I heard that we had a visitor. I'll come back for breakfast when she's gone.' She turned and left the room without either of us saying a word.

8.

I dreamt that night that Jake and I burned in our cottage, trapped by the new locks on the windows. Jake sat on a chair in the bedroom, his hands neatly placed on his knees. He was talking to me, telling me to get out, to save myself while I could. I don't know why I didn't move. People do odd things in dreams. I watched him plead with me while the flames licked at his heels and his trousers caught light. I watched the yellow and orange consume him, turning him into red blisters and then all I could see was a black hole in his face mouthing the words.

It wasn't a difficult dream to interpret when I woke up. The cottage was on fire.

I sat up quickly and coughed until my chest was sore. I heard the glass in the bedroom window smash and a rock thud onto the floor. I think another sound like that had woken me.

I was very sleepy, my brain sluggish. The room glowed very faintly orange and I could see it was hazy with thin smoke. I looked towards the door. The gap beneath it was a bright yellow slit. I panicked and got out of bed. I went straight for the window and tried to turn the handles. I was very confused when they did not move even when I flexed then, putting my full standing weight behind them.

I coughed again in the smoke and covered my face pulling up my T-shirt over my nose. I tried the handles again but still they did not move. I stared at them uncomprehending. I think it must have taken several seconds for me to focus on the shining new locks that kept me shut in. I cried out when I realised that I had left the new window keys in the kitchen.

'Lucy!' I heard someone shouting my name.
'Lucy!' It sounded like Jake's voice coming from outside the cottage. I was light-headed with the smoke. I believed he was outside.

'Move away from the window Lucy!' he said. I did what he told me, standing up and stepping backwards towards the bed. A few seconds later I heard a loud noise at the window. More panes smashed and the wooden frames creaked with the impact.

'Stay back!' he shouted. Another large object hit the window this time breaking through, snapping the cross bars on the window. A large log lay on the carpet.

'Can you get out?' the cry came from outside.

I went back to the window. One half of it was broken and it looked like I could crouch and get through it. I picked up the log and pushed out the shards of glass and remaining splinters of frame with it. I hesitated. I had flimsy moccasin slippers on my feet. I did not feel stable, slipping around in them on the window ledge.

'Lucy. You're going to have to just jump,' he said. I could hear the concern in his voice.

I heard a smashing sound below me. I suddenly couldn't see. Black smoke surrounded me. I coughed loudly and stepped back inside, unable to breathe on the window ledge. The smoke curled inwards searching for me inside the bedroom.

'Get out!' he said, his voice rising in desperation.

I took a deep breath in the rapidly deteriorating air and stepped back on to the ledge. I didn't hesitate this time. I leapt from the window not knowing or being able to see where I would land.

My body was relaxed when I landed. I'd thrown myself from the window with little hope that I would escape injury. I landed hard on my feet first. Unable to control my weight, I slumped on to my hip and my momentum kept me rolling, different parts of my body taking my weight and decelerating my fall. I felt very bruised and battered, the initial impact had resonated unpleasantly through my whole skeleton, but I did not feel anything break.

I sat on the stony floor, looking at the cottage, black smoke damping out the light of the fire inside. I felt someone put their hand around my arm, hooking me at my elbow, encouraging me away from the fire. I stood up, stumbling with fatigue and tender muscles, and let myself be led away from the cottage.

I coughed again, thick phlegm jumping and sticking in my lungs. I leant over feeling light headed again, and then crouched down. I hacked, coughing, and I felt a hand rest on my back.

I heard sirens not too far away, just short blasts getting nearer and nearer. They stopped in the direction of the top of the lane and I heard the large fire engine approach. I could see my hands in front of me in its headlights.

When I looked up I thought I saw Jake for a moment, standing over me, his hand resting on me protectively. The flashing blue lights flickered across his face. I could see him smiling at me. I blinked and the lights passed on and I saw his face change. I was horrified to recognise Ben looking down at me.

9.

    I don't remember what happened next. I don't know how badly I broke down.

    I remember Karen holding my face, saying my name to me, repeating it and looking intently into my eyes. She burst into tears when I focused on her and responded. She kissed my face, covering my cheeks and my forehead in relieved kisses.

    'Take this sweetheart,' she said. She put a pill in my mouth and then handed me a bottle of water. I obediently swallowed the high dose of Valium.

    'The doctor says your lungs sound good,' she said stroking my hair. She told me more about the state of my health but I didn't take it in. I felt comforted by her though. I liked hearing her voice, liked her stroking me.

    People talked around me, talking to Karen. They murmured around my head, but didn't seem to want to engage me. After some seconds or minutes Karen spoke to me again.

    'The doctor says you can come home with me if you like,' she said smiling at me. 'Would you like that?' she asked.

    I looked at her blankly. I think the Valium was already kicking in. I nodded. There weren't any people near us and we left the scene quietly. In retrospect I think the doctor or Karen must have cleared people away from me, especially Ben.

    We took it slowly along the lane. I was unbalanced by the medication and unsure of my footing in the torchlight. She held me tightly under my arm trying to keep me upright.

'Did they arrest Ben?' I said.

I must have asked her this before because she answered me quite calmly. 'No they didn't. He didn't start the fire,' she said squeezing my arm. 'He saved you.'

'How do you know?' I asked her, my eyes wide.

'He came here screaming his head off,' she said gently. 'He was screaming at my window to get a ladder.'

'He woke you?' I said confused.

She paused. 'No, something had woken me anyway, and I was awake. But he certainly got my attention. He ran up the lane again once he saw that I was up. He went to try and break in to get you. I think he broke your window. Whatever he did, he didn't start the fire and then try his hardest to save you,' she said.

'But what was he doing here?' I asked. My altered brain was slow but still suspicious.

She hesitated, answering it with more difficulty, her voice going a little tight as she spoke. 'He mentioned that you had an argument. He'd been trying to get through to you to apologise. I think he called round in desperation when you didn't answer his calls.'

I shook my head, not wanting to accept what she said.

'You might have had a bad argument,' she said, 'but I don't think Ben's trying to kill you,' she laughed gently as she said it, believing it ridiculous.

'But someone is,' I said quite firmly.

She was silent for a few moments. 'The police aren't sure what started the fire,' she said diplomatically. 'They're going to send over an investigator, probably tomorrow, to look at the damage and see if they can tell what started it.'

'But Ben's the only one who could have done it all,' I said frustrated that she didn't seem to be listening to me.

We had reached her front door, and she guided me through, holding my arm like I was an old lady. She closed the door behind us and locked it.

'Come upstairs,' she commanded gently. 'I need to keep an eye on you the doctor says, so I'm going to put you in my bed tonight.'

I had to concentrate on walking along the hall then up the stairs. I was feeling more and more uncoordinated, even though the floor was even and the light good now.

She put on a small lamp in her room, keeping the light low, and sat me on the side of her double bed. She sat beside me, her arm around me, squeezing my shoulder with her fingers.

My head was spinning with fatigue. I'm not sure if I slurred my words when I spoke.

'Ben's the only one who could do it,' I persisted. 'He has a key.'

'A key to what,' she said, admirably sounding interested.

'To my house,' I said as if it was obvious.

She squeezed me closer to her. 'Just because he has a key still doesn't mean he started the fire.'

I frowned, even the contraction of my forehead muscles felt as if it was happening in slow motion.

'No, not tonight.' I paused. The words were heavy in my mouth. 'The other day. Someone broke in. Needed a key.'

'Someone broke in with a key,' she said jovially to humour me.

I nodded slowly, even though I meant to vigorously.

'But other people might have a key. I think we may even have one. Mum and dad rented the cottage out before Jake persuaded them to sell it.'

I paused at what she said but didn't take in its implications. I had just enough will and brain power to press my points but nothing spare to understand anything else.

'Someone broke in. They stole T-shirt. Made me a doll, out of sack. Burnt its hair. Cut its back. Poured red on cuts. Put my T-shirt on it.' I was exhausted. 'Scared,' I said at last.

She had stopped squeezing my shoulder. 'When did this happen?' she asked quietly.

'Two days,' I said starting to droop forward, putting my elbows on my knees.

She got up slowly and walked around the room. I could see her legs moving in front of me crossing the carpet. I was too tired to lift my head to look at the expression on her face.

She knelt down in front of me and took my hands squeezing them gently together between hers. Her head was lower than mine and I could see her face. Her expression was frozen. She didn't look at me in the eyes.

'I want you to lie down now,' she said neutrally. 'I'm going out of the room for just a couple of seconds, and then I will be back,' she said. 'You're going to be quite safe here. You're quite safe now.'

She stood up and held me gently by the shoulders. She encouraged me back, lying me down in her bed. She had to lift my legs up. My limbs were too leaden for me to move them.

She pulled up the duvet, tucking it beneath my chin and kissed my forehead, leaving her lips pressed against my skin for several seconds.

I heard the door open, close and a key turning in the lock.

I don't know how long she was gone. I woke again only once. She was coming back into the room. She locked the door behind her and came and sat on the bed beside me.

'Go to sleep,' she said unable to smile. 'I will watch over you. You're safe now.'

10.

I woke with the sun shining through the bedroom window. I had to try to wake several times, my leaden eyelids snapping shut and my brain closing back down in an instant. I sat up in bed trying to force myself to stay awake. I still felt dazed and I rubbed my cheeks and forehead trying to wake my head. I guessed it was late morning by the height of the sun in the sky. I was alone in the bedroom.

I swung my legs out from under the duvet. My feet were dirty and scratched. I stared at them, waiting for my brain to unclog and explain the state of them. Images of the previous night appeared to me, out of order, jumping around. I let them settle until I understood their sequence.

I was not perturbed by the events. I remembered them quite calmly, accepting them as fact. I was interested in how my cottage looked this morning and the damage that had been caused, and I intended to go and look, but I was not too concerned. My dosed brain calmly thought that I would have to get another house.

Karen had left a set of clothes on the chair by the bed: a pair of jeans, a T-shirt, a long wool jumper and underwear. It took me a while to understand that she had left them there for me.

*

I could see her through the space between the hinges on the kitchen door and the frame. She was sitting at the table. George was sitting on her knee playing with the pterodactyl. He looked at her from time to time, but seemed to have given up on getting a response. She held her hand up to her face, her curled fingers pressed to her lips. Her brow was heavy and tight and she was staring out of the window. She was distracted and distraught. I could see that, but I didn't feel anything in response.

I pushed the door open and looked at her. I could feel my face was numb in a blank expression. She turned towards me. She tried to smile, but it just made her eyes water. She lifted George from her knee and got up to walk towards me. She fluidly put her arms around my shoulders and drew me close, squeezing her cheek against mine. She held me firmly, her chest and stomach pressed into mine, and twisted me gently from side to side. Her cheek became wet and started to stick and then slide, cool against mine.

She pulled away from me, still holding a hand around the back of my neck. She lifted her other hand and touched my face with her fingertips, gently running her finger down my cheek. She followed where her finger ran with her eyes, frowning and looking as if it caused her pain. 'I love you,' she said quietly, without being able to look me in the eye.

She dropped her hand slowly down to mine, gently taking it and leading me to the table. 'Come and have some breakfast,' she said.

She sat George back on her knee while I ate. I didn't want any food this morning. My mouth didn't crave any flavours. I felt weak though and I knew my stomach was empty, sucked in. I slowly ate and methodically chewed two pieces of toast and drank a cup of tea.

'I'm going to look at the cottage,' I said neutrally when I had finished. 'And then I'm going to work.'

She turned and looked at me, a pained expression on her face. 'There's not much left,' she said cautiously.

'But of course we can go and look if you like. She tried to smile. 'They won't be expecting you to work today darling.'

'I need to go into the office though,' I said plainly. 'I need to save the web cam images.'

She looked at me without expression. 'Web cam images?'

'I set up a small camera at the cottage after the break in. It should have caught pictures of whoever started the fire and sent a backup to my machine at work.'

She looked stunned, keeping her eyes on mine. I didn't know whether I should repeat what I said. 'I need to go into work,' I said simply.

She twitched her gaze away, but remained silent. She looked distracted, letting her head fall slightly, and stared towards the floor. Her mouth had fallen open. I didn't know what she was thinking or feeling. I took another sip of tea.

'What do you expect to find?' she asked.

'I think Ben started the fire,' I said.

She continued to stare at the floor but frowned acutely concerned. I think she had a look of despair on her face.

'You won't be convinced that he didn't do it will you?' she said more as a statement. She had tears in her eyes when she looked at me.

I didn't know what to say.

'OK then,' she said reluctantly. She stood up slowly, sliding George off her knee and steadying him up on the floor. 'We can't delay this for ever,' she said, heavy regret in her voice. 'Not even until this evening,' she added.

She stepped forward as if about to stride off and then she abruptly stopped. She put her hand to her forehead. 'How stupid,' she said out loud to herself. She turned and looked at me. 'I was about to take you in the car,' she said, looking shocked at herself.

I gulped automatically, letting what she'd said sink in, waiting for the expected panic attack. There was none. I was numb to that fear as well.

'I think that would be OK,' I said, 'if you could take me.'

*

I slept most of the way. I woke up with my head leaning against the cold window of the passenger door, rocking gently with the bumps in the road. The window was covered with condensation from my breath. It was grey outside, with a persistent drizzle. The wind-screen wipers cleaned it away intermittently. It looked as if it was a cold and miserable day.

I watched Karen drive, her slim arms and elegant hands making the unfamiliar movements, turning the steering wheel, clicking on the quiet indicators. I turned round to check on George. He was in his own small seat in the back. He was quiet today.

She turned into the car park outside my office and parked at the far end away from the entrance. She undid her seat belt when we came to a stop.

'Do you want to come in?' I asked. I thought I should have asked and then didn't know if I should.

She twitched her lips and looked at me with heavy eyes. She shook her head.

'No I'll wait here,' she said.

I started to turn to open the door when she grabbed my hand. 'Wait,' she said quietly, 'just one more minute.'

She squeezed my hands, rubbing her thumbs over my fingers, staring at them intently as if she hadn't seen them before. She drew her hand towards her face and then pressed the back of my hand to her lips. She closed her eyes while she held it there and then put my hand down again gently on my knee.

'OK,' she said, letting me go.

*

The last images copied from my computer at home were from twenty-five past eleven. I opened the last to see if it had captured the fire. It was strange seeing the familiar cottage kitchen in flames. The image was mainly white, the fire in full force as the last image was captured and the web cam melted away. I copied the last thirty minutes of images and transferred them into a player.

The kitchen appeared as normal, a static series of grey images. It was odd to think that it had gone. I watched the unchanging scene for perhaps a minute before clicking on the progress bar and dragging it forward. The frozen kitchen appeared the same for a few moments longer and then the image exploded in white as I pressed forward too quickly.

I stopped my movement and dragged the bar back, rewinding to just before the start of the fire. I clicked the next button, reviewing every image one by one.

A shape appeared at the front door. I couldn't see it clearly. It was more like a shadow. I clicked forward. The letter box was jammed open in the next one and the floor tiles had turned darker with a patch of liquid on the floor. The next image looked the same but the letter box was shut. The next was exactly the same. Two or three images later a flare of light blanked out the centre of the image. It reached high up the door and I couldn't see any details beyond it when I enlarged the area. I clicked forward again.

I could see a face. It was quite clear in the next image. The flames had died back onto the floor and were starting to gently lap at the foot of the kitchen cabinets and burn through the mat by the door. The face hadn't been where I was looking for it. I had been enlarging an area near the top of the door. The face was just over half way up. It looked down at the fire with large eyes, in awe of the fire taking hold. It smiled. I'd never seen Sophia look so pleased.

I was shocked, but I didn't feel it. I stared at the image. The reality started to settle slowly, my mind making connections, the truth when made obvious melting in with such clarity that I couldn't deny it.

Everything fitted. You know when something's right. She'd had the time. I could imagine that she hated me with enough vitriol to imagine her slashing away at my image and delivering that doll with pleasure. I didn't doubt that she wished me burned in the cottage.

She must have recognised her mother's preference immediately, before even she did, digging that hole in the path so that I might injure myself and stop running past the house. It was funny in a way. I almost enjoyed the irony in my numb state. It must have been quite frustrating for her how things kept playing out. Almost everything she had done and my reaction to it had pushed me closer to Karen, sent me running to her. It couldn't have gone any worse for her, until now.

I sat staring at the photo, wondering what would happen now. I played out every scenario I could imagine. I was quite rational in my state. I could evaluate each future story quite without passion, allowing myself to imagine other people's emotions, their guilt, their ties, without being distracted by my own.

I came to my conclusion without pain, but realising I would find it agonising later. I dragged the cursor around the folders of backed up images, highlighting them all, and then pressed the delete button on the keyboard.

*

I didn't say anything to Karen when I sat back in the car. I looked up at her silently for a moment. It was all she needed for her suspicions to be confirmed. She turned away and put her hand to cover her eyes. But I could see her mouth open beneath it. The sides of her mouth creased and turned down as if hooks were pulling them. A drop of saliva started to run in a colourless string. She started to shake and convulse and she breathed in noisily in a sob that shook her chest.

I looked away. I couldn't feel a thing.

Part 6
1.

They were looking at me. They never stopped looking. I couldn't lift my head to catch their gazes over the top of the supermarket shelves. I stared at the shelf in front of me. I looked at the tins of sauces, soups and beans. I couldn't decide what to have. I didn't have an appetite to eat anything much these days. I cowered behind the shelves, weighed down. I felt the grip in the centre of my chest that I felt everyday and wished I could curl up and hide on the shelf and go to sleep.

I breathed out and grabbed a can of food at random and put it in the shopping basket.

'House fire,' I heard someone say quietly from the other side of the store.

'So sad. Lost everything,' I heard someone else say, her voice thick with pity.

They had no idea.

I paid in cash at the till. I put out my hand, silently holding a note. Middle-aged, puffy fingers took it and passed me several cold coins in return. I didn't have the energy to lift my head to look at the woman at the till. She would have expected me to have smiled, acknowledging the change she had given me and acknowledging that she recognised who I was. I put the cans of food in my rucksack and strode out of the door, looking at my feet.

I'd moved up to the house near Ben's. It was only a few hundred metres from the supermarket. I reached home within five minutes, not even far enough to work up a sweat and feel the adrenaline invigorate me.

I opened the front door into my new, brick house. I stepped through the door and threw the keys on the hard laminate floor. The keys echoed noisily around the empty white interior. I had few possessions beyond those that Ben had scraped together when I'd moved in a few weeks ago.

The kitchen had a new kettle, two mugs, two plates, two of every piece of cutlery. Ben had split his own possessions to help me get by. The dining room remained bare, its door permanently shut. I had Ben's old sofa and portable TV in the living room. I spent almost all of my time in that room. I hardly went upstairs. There was a mattress on the floor in the bedroom, but I tended to fall asleep in front of the TV at some time early in the morning most days.

I put my bag on the floor in the sitting room and sat on the sofa, turning on the TV out of habit. I stared at it. The news was on. Half focusing I watched the pictures of chaos flash by not taking any of it in.

I had been signed off from work. The doctor had been quite happy, eager even, that I take some time off. I'm not sure if it was the best thing for me. I had very little structure to my day. If I'd closed the curtains and thrown out the clocks, it would have had very little impact on my life. I spent hours staring at the TV, and more and more hours sleeping in front of it. The less I did the more lethargic and apathetic I became.

I never went running anymore. The thought of it, taking my old route past Karen's house, would fill me with sorrow. Tears would start to flow coldly from my eyes. All the energy would disappear from my legs and I would begin to shake before I'd even taken a step from the house.

I saw her in Pennance one day. She hardly came into the village it seemed. She stopped outside the post office when I was leaving the supermarket. I was already on the other side of the green when she pulled up in the car. She didn't see me when she got out. I stood, two shopping bags in my hands, staring at the car.

I could see Sophia in the front. She was talking to someone on her pink mobile phone, laughing at something they said to her. She didn't notice me staring at the car. I could see the shape of George on the back seat. He was in the middle, in darkness. I couldn't see him clearly through the condensation on the window. He didn't seem to be moving, just sitting quietly. I wanted to know how he was, whether he still liked the pterodactyl I gave him.

I knew it was time to turn away but I found I couldn't move. I could feel the weight of the shopping weighing me down to the spot, my legs stiff and unmovable, my eyes locked onto the car. My body only twitched when Karen came out of the post office.

I felt foolish then, staring hopelessly at her car and child. I couldn't take my eyes away from her when she looked at me. She half looked, not quite focusing and gave me a half smile, her mouth pinching in the corners; the kind of distracted look that she gave me when we first met. She only glanced at me for a moment, not even long enough to interrupt her movement from the post office to the car door. She didn't turn around to look again when she drove away. I would have seen her. I stayed frozen to the spot watching her car pull away, turn down the lane towards the sea and disappear past the last houses.

2.

I stepped out of the house one day. I'd lost track of time and it was dark outside. It was full moon. It must have been the second since the fire. I think it was very early in the morning. A frost had coated everything and the road and houses sparkled in the orange street lights.

It was peaceful. No-one was around. I started to walk out of the cul-de-sac. It was refreshing not to have to lower my gaze to avoid other people's looks of pity and curiosity. There was no-one to spy on my movements or talk about me.

I stood for a moment when I reached the green. It was quiet. I could hear the sea. I'd never heard it in Pennance before. There had always been the background hum of cars, the whirr of air conditioning from shops, and the chatter of people to drown out its faint hush.

I started to walk, out of the village, along the familiar road towards the cottage.

The moonlight was strong, reflecting off the frost-covered fields. I could see quite clearly in the light. I had a long thin shadow bent in a sharp angle across the road and up into the hedge.

The sheep in the fields were lying down, their heads held up stiffly, as if they were frozen solid on the grass. They did not turn as I passed by.

*

I hadn't seen the cottage since it had been cleared and the police tape had been taken away. I stared at the burned-out shell, letting my eyes adjust to the dimmer light under the trees. I approached the black gaping hole that had been the front door and leaned on the wall to peer in. It felt cold and sticky. I looked at my hand and felt the wet greasy soot between my thumb and fingers, dark on my pale hands.

I leaned through the doorway. The roof and first floor had collapsed. The burned remains of the bedroom lay in a heap in what had been the kitchen. I didn't dare enter. I couldn't see the ground clearly enough to tread safely. I didn't need to inspect much more thoroughly to see that Ben had been accurate in his description. There was nothing left of the cottage, none of my belongings.

There was no trace of Jake. All his clothes that had been left in the wardrobe, all his old school books in the grey cardboard boxes, his shoe box of photographs were all cremated. It was difficult to imagine him in this blackened shell of our home. I regretted not sorting his belongings out then. I had nothing to remember him by. I did not want my memory of the photograph of him in the Alps to fade. I tried to remember it clearly as I stood there, trying to embed it into my mind to stop it from losing its detail.

I'd always intended sharing his things out between Ben and Margaret. I would have kept a few things. But they would have liked the photos I think.

'I'm sorry,' I said out loud apologising to him. But it didn't feel like he haunted the cottage anymore and I don't think he heard.

I didn't miss the cottage. I felt sorry that it had been burned as I would any other old building, but I didn't feel a sharp loss at its dereliction. I'd been so unhappy there that it was almost a relief that my existence couldn't continue within it. I'd missed the sound of the sea though. I found myself wandering along the lane following its inhalation and then whisper up the valley.

 I walked slowly underneath the trees until the lane started to widen and the valley opened out by the manor. I looked out to the mercurial sea, glistening in the moonlight. I closed my eyes, breathing in time with it, the air chilling my lungs in cool waves.

 I opened my eyes and turned round to look at the house, to check that no-one could see me. The windows were dark, the house's pale face quiet and asleep. I looked at Karen's bedroom window. I could picture her clearly, sleeping under the white duvet in her bed, her dressing gown thrown over the back of the chair by the bed. I imagined her pale face relaxed in the moonlight, dark strands of hair curling across her cheek. I could still remember her smell, could imagine leaning close into her, feeling her warmth against my face, inhaling her aroma.

 My chest tightened and my forehead tensed. I couldn't indulge too often in these images, extending my memory of her into my present. They comforted me and then choked me, making me feel her loss as acutely as I had the first time.

 I looked over the house again, taking in all its details; the number of windows, the plants that stood frozen outside the front door. I did not intend coming back again now that I had seen the cottage. It was too painful being this close to Karen. I did not think I could trust myself not to slip one day, bang on her door, begging her to take me in despite all the problems that it would entail.

 I turned away, inhaling sharply. My eyes had started to water, the tears turning icy cold as they ran down my face. I wiped them away quickly, as if hiding them from someone who was watching me.

    I walked back up the lane unable to tolerate the torturous surroundings anymore. I didn't look back. I walked quickly and determined back to the village. I worked up a sweat, my chest feeling raw with the exertion. I was almost smiling with the high from the exercise when I reached the village green.

    I stopped for a moment, to recover my breath. Opposite the post office on the edge of the green was Jake's memorial bench. I laughed when I saw it. I hadn't realised that Margaret had purchased it and laid it out. I hadn't seen her much since the fire. I think I had Ben to thank for deflecting her visits.

    I had to smile at her memorial though now as I approached it. It was the only thing there was to remind me of Jake. And the funny thing was that I could imagine him sitting there. Now the cottage was burned down, I could imagine him haunting the village green instead, taking a rest from his ghostly walks on the bench.

    It looked crisp and grey in the moonlight. I stroked away the crystals on the seat and sat down, the coolness seeping through my trousers immediately. I put my arm across the back and touched the shining plaque. *Jake Arundell, much loved.* I ran my fingers around the letters of his name, writing it out.

    I smiled again. I wondered, amused, if he had any advice for recovering from having a heart broken by Karen. I found it difficult to imagine them as a couple. I supposed that it had been a long time ago and that people change. I wanted to know what Jake had been like when he was that age, when he had met Karen. I missed him suddenly. I wanted to talk to him. I missed his company.

It wasn't out of guilt. I didn't miss him out of duty. I wanted to talk to him. I wanted his advice. I wanted to laugh with him. I wanted to laugh at how ironic it was that I had fallen in love with the same woman that he had. I wanted him to take my hand and squeeze it, turning to me to laugh, his big barrel of a chest moving in and out as he talked to me with that comforting deep voice.

'I miss you Jake Arundell' I said fondly, tracing around his name again. 'I really miss you.'

3.

I think I had decided that I should leave Pennance before she even called. She telephoned on a Sunday. I remember that quite clearly. I was meeting Ben for Sunday lunch at the pub later that morning.

'Hello?' I answered the call cautiously.

'Hi.'

I knew it was her straight away, her clear voice recognisable over the distortion of the phone. She had only said one word but it carried such regret and hurt while remaining calm, apologetic almost.

'Hi,' I said plainly. Her voice had made me freeze, a reminder of what I had lost cutting straight through me. We were both silent. All I heard was the buzz of the phone.

'How are you?' she asked. She tried to sound polite, as if her question was a formality, not really delving too deeply, but I could hear she wanted to know how I had been coping. I wondered if she knew how much I had missed her. I wondered if she wanted to hear how much I missed her.

'I'm fine thanks,' I replied quietly after a few moments. I had to swallow. My voice was starting to crack. I gulped down the lump in my throat.

'I was wondering if you would like to come over for lunch today?' she asked gently. She sounded hesitant, almost embarrassed.

It took me by surprise. I hadn't expected it, even though I had longed for her to call, even though I knew she couldn't, shouldn't.

'It would just be me and George,' she added reassuring. And then quietly 'We've missed you very much.'

It was too much. I had to cover the phone so that she couldn't hear my breathing become harsh with the tears that had started to flow. I sniffed and cleared my throat, blinking back the tears before trying to talk again.

'I, I can't today, sorry. I'm meeting Ben,' I said shakily.

'We'd like you to come another day if you can't make today. Any day would be fine for us,' she said softly.

I covered my mouth. I imagined seeing her, opening the door, putting her arms out to greet me. Would I be able to simply hug her in return, without breaking down, without pleading with her? Would I be able to sit with her, as pleasant company, while my heart broke realising that I could never reach out and touch her, never lean across and kiss her bare neck where her T-shirt slipped down her shoulder?

I breathed in, shuddering with a sob. 'I, I don't think that's a good idea. I'm sorry... I can't.' I put the phone down before my sorrow became too audible, cutting her off.

I was disappointed with my reaction. I'd assumed that I would be able to talk to her as a friend. I'd imagined myself wanting to act cordially, eager to have her company if she offered it when Sophia was not around. I'd thought that I would be able to control my sorrow so that I could still enjoy her friendship.

But I felt such overwhelming loss when I heard her voice, her calm tones that flowed over me and right through me, tantalising. I wanted her. I wanted to be with her and I could think of nothing else when I heard her. My whole body ached wishing it could hold her, lay with her, just feel her close, the warmth of her skin next to mine. I wanted nothing else. I couldn't think of ever craving anything else but her. I could have cried out with the frustration I felt.

She texted later. 'Please call if you change your mind. I'll understand if you don't want to. Love K.' I stared at the message. I closed it. Then I opened it again to re-read it, to concentrate on how she had signed off with love. I shook my head, feeling the tears and unbearable longing build inside every time I re-read her message.

*

'You OK?' Ben asked concerned.

I was still visibly upset when he called round. I shook my head telling him not to worry, picking up my keys and closing the front door behind me.

He took my arm, hooking his elbow under mine as we walked towards the green. 'You don't look OK,' he said frowning.

'No I'm fine,' I said trying to smile. 'Karen phoned, that's all,' I said a little embarrassed.

'What did she say?' he asked after a pause.

'Not very much. I, I couldn't talk to her. I put the phone down.' My voice was starting to fracture again.

He didn't say anything. He looked down at me kindly, pursing his lips, trying to offer a stoic smile.

*

We sat in the snug around the back of the pub. It was quite busy that day. Everyone perhaps needed cheering up with a warm Sunday lunch. Ben sipped at his pint and looked at the menu. I stared at my copy, reading the options over and over, not registering them.

'Did you see the bench on the green?' he asked absently, still looking at the menu. 'Do you like it?'

It took me a few seconds to realise what he referred to. 'Oh yes. Actually I do,' I said smiling. 'It reminded me of him the other day. It was good. Good to remember him.'

Ben smiled at me, agreeing.

We fell silent again, and studiously looked at the menus.

'What you having then?' Ben asked looking up at me.

I couldn't think. I wasn't even hungry. I breathed in and out deeply. 'I don't know. What you having?' I said putting the menu back down on the table.

'Roast beef for me,' he said, smiling in anticipation of his lunch.

'Same for me then,' I said not wanting to hold the order up.

I was still staring at the table when Ben came back from ordering the food. He waved his hand beneath my face to break my trance.

'Sorry,' I said smiling.

He didn't say anything, patiently letting me continue if I chose to.

'I think I should move,' I said. 'I think I should move away.'

He looked surprised and disappointed at the same time, but didn't stop me from talking.

'It's too painful here,' I said looking away. 'It's only you that's keeping me here now,' I said, not wanting to dismiss his kindness over the previous weeks.

He nodded his head down in acknowledgement and looked at the table. 'Where will you go?' he asked.

'I don't know. London for a while at least. Then I'll have to think after that.'

'Not London. You love the countryside,' he said appalled. He bit his tongue, and then smiled resigned.

I tried to smile back at him. I took a sip of my pint, just as something to do to fill the silence. He looked uncomfortable, shy almost. He looked as if he was going to say something but didn't know whether he should. He leaned forward, reaching across the table, taking my hand and holding it for a few moments. He looked into my eyes and squeezed my hand, before withdrawing his arm back across the table.

'I saw Karen the other day,' he said.

I twitched at him mentioning her name out loud and tried to keep my composure. I could only nod for him to continue.

'The divorce has gone through now. Sounds like it was unpleasant. She didn't say so outright like, but I can't imagine her husband made it easy for her.'

I nodded again. I didn't want to picture Karen upset, or how her husband may have treated her. It would have drawn tears from me within seconds.

'David's taken custody of Sophia,' he said lightly, picking up his pint and taking a sip.

My mouth dropped open a little, my thoughts trying to escape. I looked at him.

'Is she OK? Is she OK about losing Sophia?' I couldn't help asking keenly.

He shrugged. 'I wouldn't say she was happy. More resigned to it I suppose.' He looked away trying to recall. 'She seemed to think it was for the best. Better for George anyway, I think she said. I think there was some trouble there,' he said looking at me questioningly.

I couldn't say anything. My heart was beating so strongly I felt my hand lift to my chest to try to calm it. I had to turn away from him. My eyes were wide and my face flushed as I was suddenly allowed to indulge in all the possibilities this opened up.

What had she intended this morning when she phoned? Did she want to be friends, the pain of the past too much for anything more? Or did she still feel the way she did before the fire? I couldn't stop my mind from racing ahead.

I looked at Ben. My legs were twitching, impatient to leave, wanting to run to see Karen.

He smiled resigned. 'I'll tell them to hold your lunch,' he said.

I leapt up, leaning across the table to kiss him on the forehead. I held his cheek. 'Thank you,' I said, realising what a difficult admission it had been for him.

*

I had to stop myself from running down the lane towards the manor house. My legs felt light and trembled. It felt as if I had hardly any control over them. I had to hold back my emotions, not let my hope overwhelm me. I needed to face her calmly and rationally so that I could accept what she wanted from me.

I could see my hand shaking as I reached up for the door bell. I stepped back two paces from the door, not wanting to be too close to her so that she might see my underlying feelings. I had to force myself to breathe more calmly as I heard her footsteps coming nearer the door.

I had my speech ready, my excuses. I was just passing, wondering if I could change my mind about that lunch one day. I breathed in ready to say it as she opened the door.

The air escaped from me silently when I saw her. I could feel my face change. I could feel that I was looking at her with hope so obviously spread across my face. I started to tear up at the thought that it was hopeless and had to look down, unable to face her rejection.

I saw her step towards me out of the corner of my eye. I saw her body come close to mine as she lifted her arms around my shoulders. I could feel her warmth as she enveloped me. She pulled my head towards her chest and held me close under her chin. I couldn't speak as she lifted my face towards her, couldn't open my eyes to look at her, scared of what I would see. I felt her soft lips kiss my cheeks, my wet tears, and slowly cover every inch of my face.

Acknowledgements

Many thanks to Jayne Fereday, Ceri Lloyd and Mike Ashton for vital feedback and encouragement.

About the author

Find out more about the author and her work at: http://rclareashton.wordpress.com

Printed in Great Britain
by Amazon